San Bernardino, Singing

www.InlandiaInstitute.org
First Edition

San Bernardino, Singing

Edited by Nikia Chaney

Inlandia Books

Contents

Youth Writing

About *San Bernardino, Singing*

Foreword
San Bernardino, Singing

I came to San Bernardino at the age of 17. I had just gotten married. I traveled with my new husband from South Central Los Angeles all the way to San Bernardino on the bus. All of the seats had blue cloth on them, and I was fascinated at how expensive they seemed compared to LA's hard tan plastic. Looking out the windows I felt like I was going to some far-off land, like my teenaged life had been intervened by some fairy godmother.

And what did this fantasy land look like?

Desert, everywhere. I had never seen the desert before. All around me were mountains that cut through the sky to stand like cinnamon walls at the horizon. Houses had yards that seemed stretched out, like a giant hand had slowly erased the sidewalks and set each house further apart. We lived in Muscoy right off Highland on a street that was bulldozed years ago to make room for the entrance to the 210 freeway. From the east windows, nothing but brush and scrub, brown-gold grass and rocks that hid the city highways from view as if that house were at the edge of the world.

I felt small in that little house with its chickens and wild dogs and leaning gates. I would listen to the Santa Ana winds rattling the doorways, homesick for Inglewood, and wonder why I was here, what was this strange rural city and what did it ask of me.

I did not know then the power of place, how a town and county can seep into the body through the eyes and ears like second-hand smoke or distant drums or perfume or sand under the feet.

All of my children were born here in San Bernardino. When I think of

San Bernardino, I think of taking my children with me to the laundromat on Del Rosa or the 99 Cent store on E. I think of how my son was born in the parking lot of the old county hospital on Gilbert, and that time I found myself enrolled on a whim at San Bernardino Valley College, scared and naïve but so earnest and ready to learn. A professor there told me to write poetry and years later I would tell my own students to do the exact same thing at CSUSB, in workshops, in grocery stores.

How could I not love a place that gave me voice and taught me how to write?

When asked to represent the Inland Empire as the Literary Laureate for 2016-2018, I knew I wanted to do something for San Bernardino. It was and it is still so important for me to have something tangible for San Bernardino, to honor it and speak its name.

One of the beauties of any anthology is the multiplicity of voices. In gathering work, I was always constantly amazed at how the people of San Bernardino see this city and county. These words and images in these pages reflect a place and history that is just as rich and varied as my own memories and experiences. For those passing through and those who call it home, San Bernardino and its history, its gold desert and its mahogany mountains, always sings.

Nikia Chaney, 2020

Love Song For Bobby Soto
Orlando Ramirez

I guess you have to be an alcoholic to understand, he
said by way of passing. I guess, I replied, wondering
if this tragic romanticism accrued to all alcoholics or
just the artistic ones.

We were driving down Mount Vernon, sitting way up
in his big truck like kings surveying the botanicas, the
carnecerias the llanterias painted yellow and fuschia
and fussy cobalt blue.

The sun shone so white it hurt, oscillating, breaking.
The surge and crest and retreat, a worry like a Phillip
Glass song played by the Kronos Quartet dosed on two
grams of methamphetamine.

The sawing up and down, the spiking heat and the blue
notes of the soundtrack were the peaks and valleys of
a startled afternoon dragging the rest of a day like a sack
of rusted auto parts.

This is where we are. Buzzards dressed like Realtors
circling above the humble scavengers of change,
mauling the carrion of family court, hiding thousands
in their secret bank accounts.

The blue-black lizards, the crows dyed ochre and silver,
the cotton blossoms of concern trudging, trailing

shopping baskets full of burning newspapers down the
length of the shimmering avenue.

I said, You got to hand it to the human spirit. Even with
the war going on and all the other crap, people still open
up their tienditas, their quinceañera shops, their places to
sell piñatas for a kid's birthday,

You fool, he laughed. These businesses are all just fronts.
In the back they're laundering money or they got some
mojaditos held hostage, guarded by coyotes in exchange
for two thousand ransom.

I guess, I said, as we passed a church where a short line
of white cars idled in front of the vestibule. The drivers
in white shirts and black vests waited, wiped the sweat
from the back of their necks.

You guess? He laughed. You guess? Though they hissed
like wasps trapped in the cab of the truck, I let the taunts
go. I had to. Their sting would only have been amplified
by the weak swat of my reply.

I guess, I said again, knowing I'd be judged by the harsh
teleology, but I refused to burrow into the low cynicism of
these times, give teeth to the lie, lip the lispy Heil Hitler
to explain the irrational cruelty

that finds its way, passing through the anesthetized cities
the way alcoholics pass shoe polish and paint thinner

through white bread to distill the anxiety and keep the
spirits strong.

When we die and go to heaven, will we still be together?
It's a song he sings when he is worried. He doesn't mean
me and him, he means somebody else or nobody else or
else he means just himself.

He sang it then and I pictured us riding high in his F-250
on streets paved with gold, the angel gangs toking on
the corners where the placas on the walls all looked like
lost Siqueiros and Basquiats.

Heaven, he says, is just like the farm. The fence is easy
enough to climb, but nobody ever does. If you do, then
they add another five years. It's not worth it, he says,
And I'm sure never going back.

Crossroads Acrostic for Fault Crossing Metropolis
Julie Sophia Paegle

Speeding down the Cajon Pass, we swerve into swelter and the city sees us. And so, no longer
anonymous, we are heat seized. Crosshairs rise up unbidden within us, not quite a presence,
neither a transparence, nor the twilight opacities of cities spilled into each other across sundown

Boundaries. Left, tracks; right, alluvial fans drift northwest from the rest of America, which
eases southeast along with river's end, past wherever waters slow enough from their mouth's
roaring torrents to drop rough blocks of terrains scraped off the far part of mountain range. Say
no place like home, say no way to see, say how hard we push to merge our bodies to drop bulky
ampersands from *you & me.* We've pulled over to pull at each other by the rocks where your bullet
razed the Muledeer buck heaving his five by five rack wrought from forage free to grow from seeds
dropped into ash mud of the Blue Cut Fire's clear-cut. He laid down his burden. His velvet ends
in us, fixed. Give me your hand, some weight. Our stars might yet antler across onyx. Let's go down
now, to love's grind & crush, to city that spans our frictions & faults even when we shove past each
other, Pedro & Padre, la Llorona & Jedediah, syringe slip orange seed hoax polis coaxing need full
stop open mouth kiss into an adult buck's velvet night, shed at Santa Ana's hiss: *cut your horns on this.*

At the End of the Devil's Breath
Romaine Washington

So much blood slicked the floor you had to be careful not to fall. The explosion of guns, blood puddled thick… listening to the first responder I get stuck in tears trying to wrap my mind around it - my thoughts in a knotted loop - - don't know what to say - don't know anyone who was killed or injured or related to someone who was, but I feel like I do.

Mom and I drove by that area last week on the way to Costco on Hospitality Lane. It's one of the nicer looking areas in San Bernardino – and now this.

None of it makes sense. Terror attack – mass shooting to make a political statement? We are one of the top thirty deadliest cities, so why target a place that is already shell shocked, steeped in murder and despair?! What political statement are they making? Not a tourist attraction – no military base here… nothing but gang wars and…

I heard one reporter say that the couple was living the American Dream. Not sure I know what that means anymore. A house, job, car, child and the appearance of a happy marriage – is just that – appearances. Not only that, take those appearances and place them in San Bernardino, a city similar to Compton, economically depressed, closed stores and job opportunities – doesn't sound like a dream. Now take that family, move them to the Hamptons and it looks more like a dream, with more to lose and more of a political statement to be made – but here?

When this happened, I realized I wanted San Bernardino to be known for something good. Before this – it was just a place I came from - struggled through and tried to forget. December 2nd brought snapshots of childhood rituals framed by the voice and eyes of my mother.

She came from a farm town in Ohio and would tell me that when she and my dad moved here she thought they were in hell. No greenery, clouds of dirt, tumbleweeds, dry hot desert air – the middle of nowhere is how she put it. Only temporary she thought. Hard to believe that in 1977 the National Civic League gave it the title of All American City.

Westside, San Bernardino neither looks nor behaves the way it did when I was growing up. Back then it was a friendly, safe, spacious yet closely knit community; an idyllic desert Mayberry RFD. From what my mom tells me, the practice of redlining (segregated housing) was legal. She was always in cuss mode when she talked about it. When in a good mood she would put a spin on it and describe where we lived as an elite upper class African-American community. The main street was Magnolia and it was lined with beautiful trees. She said our neighborhood was called:

Magnolia Estates
Romaine Washington

We bought our Kentucky

Blugreen lawns

Toepleasng plush / precision mowed

Drill sergeant edged to side/

              Walk underneath bowing Magnolias

                      Redlined

        Westcoast Westside San Bernardino

                      Redlined

      Jim crowed / we cawed beyond sheethoodedneighbors

        We bundled ourselves away from and into

        Kinship of upper-segregated – negro – we proud

                Doctors-lawyers- teachers-preachers

                    Ebony – blueblood

        Barrier breaking

        But boxed in obsidian

                    Redlined

My father was a Major in the Army, who survived two wars, but died of a heart attack while mowing the lawn. I don't know if he had chest pains or felt tired before it happened - I was too young. But I do know that community accountability and aesthetics were important to both my dad Mack and mom Betty. We lived on M — — — Street, which some might refer to as a dead end - she reimagined it by strategically planting bushes and referring to it with a more sophisticated word.

Cul-de-sac is French
Romaine Washington

The bottom of a purse
      Possibly
      Loose change
      Possibility
      Of change
      Turn around
            Come out

From bottom
Framed in barbed wire
The crisscross stop of steel
      Redlined

Uprooted
      She plants
      A laughing bush
      A pretty tease of poison
      Of pink and white
         Oleanders
A redlined ultimatum
Death is a bottomless black

But she believes in
      Balance

Plants Italian Cypress
In between Oleanders
Evergreen finger
Pointing skyward

Taller than
Pink and white blooms,
Barbed wire fences,

Our eyes travel upward
Recognizing hope
When we see it.

The beauty of our yard was meant to inspire us to move beyond the redline and I joined my mom in this pretty rebellion with bi-monthly chores of cutting the hedges and raking the yard.

This coupled with the visual freedom of the farm next to where we lived excited my imagination for the future and past. From the earthy smell of hay, lazy summer afternoons of watching horses and cows graze, and western TV shows, I not only lived on the Westside but in the Wild West.

Back at the Ranch
Romaine Washington

When your neighbor is a farm
You are on a farm.
In the Wild West
Lean Lucas McCain
Stridin' down the middle
Of a lonesome road.
Wolf-eyed, stoic aim,
Hip level-rapid fire
Rifleman,
Ready to protect
Town folk.
While his son,
Mark and I,
Milk cows and
Wait for "Pa".

When your neighbor is a farm
You are on a farm.
Gallopin' into town
On a wild brown horse,
Marshal Matt Dillon
Keepin' Miss Kitty
Safe, with his *Gunsmoke*
Cowboy hat in hand.

Cowgirl
Pushing bedtime
At sundown.
TV looks like
Campfire.

When your neighbor is a farm
You are on a farm.
Harmonica and,
Theme song sing along:

"We chased lady luck,
'til we finally struck
Bonanza
…With a horse and a saddle,
And a range full of cattle…"

Adam, Hoss, Little Joe and Will,
Ben Cartwright and me
Ridin' against
A backdrop
Of mountains.
Could be Paramount.
Back at the ranch.

No settlement in the Wild West would be complete without a Catholic Mission. St. Anthony – the patron saint of lost and stolen things – was located on the corner of Western and 16th Street. It was a small chalk-white church that smelled of frankincense and old wood, to the front was a large two-story convent and behind it a row of nine warm pink-brick classrooms. All the nuns wore long black habits with big-beaded rosaries like lassos hanging from their waists.

Uniformly they made sure we understood our mission of earning all A's in every subject; no sports teams, ASB, class presidents or clubs. While public school kids bonded, from kindergarten through eighth, I was an outsider walking my own private terrain to the library.

Up Magnolia Street, absorbing the shade of the trees that hover above - turn right on a street whose name I can't recall, where a small house transformed into a public library stood. Today, I think, that nameless street has been changed to Medical Center Drive– maybe.

Memory is a Map Rezoned
Romaine Washington

Archivist:
Mary Mcleod Bethune Library?
Never existed.

Summer Reader's Club
Never existed?
My African-American
Heroine of academics,
Entrepreneur, philanthropist,
Mary Mcleod Bethune
Library did not exist?

Archivist:
No. Mary Kellogg Library
Was the name.

Flakes of memory freefall from
Girl with bird wing braids
Staring at Bethune in an oval frame.

   When the Civil Rights Act became a reality, black flight took hold of the neighborhood. Friends and neighbors began to move away and many of the black businesses that had been supported by the community - closed. By the 1980's, as the neighborhood slowly dissembled, even the largest, most successful black owned businesses went under. It was still mainly a quiet peaceful place but there were corner guys who hung around waiting and watching.

Our home was broken into during the night while we were asleep. Afterwards, mom put dead bolts on the doors and grills on the windows. The bars were the beginning of feeling protected from the world yet shut out at the same time. I realized that we were no longer living in the mystique of the open Wild West, but the stigma of the crime riddled Westside.

We moved to M— — — Street in Rialto in hopes of recapturing the carefree sense of safety and optimism. The grills and locks went up immediately so it seemed like there was no change at all. Being my last year at San Bernardino High School, I decided to commute, sometimes walking four miles to school and wearily walking another four miles back home sometimes catching the city bus.

Close to the end of the commuting days - there was a stabbing on the bus. We had a white driver who was the size of Barney Fife who wanted the guys in the back to turn down their music. He stopped the bus, in the projects, walked to the back to "handle the boys." He was stabbed. It would be the last time I saw him driving the bus but it wouldn't be the last time we encountered each other.

From Bus to Badge
Romaine Washington

Boom box heroes before
Radio Raheem and Do the Right Thing
Leroy an'em lookin' like
They would murder for fun,
Claim territory in Rosa Parks' reject.

White shirt, small frame,
Lookin' like sweat didn't know his name.
In the middle of the projects he parks.
Orders Leroy an'em to kill the sound
Or get off.

Bus dies quiet as police take names.
Leroy an'em gone.
Soundless except for flies
Hovering over
Stabbed beads of blood.

Tension between cops and the black community was and still is high.
They used to harass kids by giving tickets for spitting on the sidewalk... I
don't mean spitting at someone, but just spitting when you need to. Usually this would happen at the bus stop, at the Carousel Mall which time has
disintegrated.

Carousel Mall
Romaine Washington

Have a fun time while doing your shopping
Have such a fun time Central City Mall
Central City Mall

The Mall that has it all

Have a fun time
this is what a mall crypt sounds like
rattling gates of steel teeth echoing
in a gaping mouth
no one to feed it
nothing to feed it
jan
i
tors
shuf
fle
a
bout
as

though

there
is

some

thing
to
clean
a lonely radio station
sits in the corner

gone

bookstore where i worked my first job
upstairs store where i bought my prom dress
jeweler where he bought our gold ring
regal African clothes and things
i dreamed of buying one day

gone

the wooden bench
where we sat
people watching
is still there
but no one to watch
no reason to sit
pastel unicorns frozen in time
encircled by a kiddie train
too tired to make one more round
without passengers

The mall was one of many economic casualties of change that occurred in 1994 when Norton Air Force Base was deactivated. It had been a mainstay in the area since WWII when it was established to protect Los Angeles from a possible attack after Pearl Harbor. The Base Realignment and Closure left San Bernardino unprotected from financial fall out. We were slowly becoming a west coast variation of Detroit. Even the headquarters for Campus Crusade for Christ, which was located in the Arrowhead mountains abandoned us.

San Bernardino, 1994

Romaine Washington

Sometimes the desert
Gets tired of being deserted.
Gets tired of itself.

We are working on
Forgetting our name.
Anguished bird throat

Tries to pull us up
Into protest,
But the sun has baked us

Frozen and weary.
Faded gray, gouged roads,
Weeds choke ankles.

Steel spike fences,
Black barred windows,
Prisoned by smog,

Bankrupt, base closed
Planes soar
Into a breathless sky.

White flight – black flight,
Blight of emptiness.
Pit bulls pace scorched yards
Daring to break free.

A decade of travel brought me back to a city I no longer recognized. Billboards covered in graffiti. Businesses boarded up and many storefronts were converted to churches for Blacks and Hispanics on the Westside. The Mary Kellogg Library is now the Lost and Found Church with the scripture Luke 15:24 *For this son of mine was dead and alive again; he was lost and is found...* Houses of faith have replaced most of the businesses, banks and fast food restaurants. Ghettos are well-established. Even the once coveted condo complexes in Highland have been appointed the title *Little Africa*.

Descent
Romaine Washington

First it was the leaving.
He sucked salutes of
Respectability from us,

A woman ravished,
Lover disappeared,
Too many children to feed.

They scamper away
To find a means to an end

And that end

Is a mean way to die;
Drug traffic replaced
Airplane traffic.

Guns proliferated.

We all know
Someone
Who has been
Murdered.
We all know
Someone
Who is struggling
To live.

In 1999, I began teaching at Pacific High School with many of the high risk students enrolled in my classes. When I asked one of the students to create his family tree he drew his gang family and shared in detail and eagerness monikers and birth names. During lunch time, in the back of the school, boys were being jumped into gangs with the illusion of being transformed into men. One day a student asked to come home with me out of fear that gang members were going to kill him for not joining.

Boxed In
Romaine Washington

If I leave
They will kill me
Slowly and mercilessly
Like a tortured ant.
I will be squashed
Between the cracks
On some isolated sidewalk
On the wrong side
Of the city.
Knuckles
Pressed in
On my brain.
The silence of dead bodies
Is floating around us,
Filling up the room,
Boxing us in.
The bell has rung.
The mad asphalt
Is rising up.
Waiting
I am
For you
To take me with you.
I
Will not die
Alone.

Within the three years that I worked at Pacific it went from being an open campus to a facility with chain link fences to cordon off different sections. With the erection of fences, more fights broke out and riots erupted; it felt like preparations for prison.

Pacific was once one of the preferred high schools to attend in San Bernardino. Now, ninety-one percent of the students are designated as low income. In 2010 it was listed as one of the seven worst schools in California.

In 2014 and '15 San Bernardino had the infamous distinction of being listed as one of the top thirty cities with the highest murder rate. From the Westside Mayberry RFD to an I.E. Straight Outta Compton - population of 216,018 people.

This is not the Twin Towers where the population in New York City is 8.55 million people. San Bernardino is no longer reminiscent of anything quaint but there is a ruggedness of Wild West survival and hope.

Despite the tragedies and hardships, the fault lines and earthquakes, bankruptcy and statistics, withered lawns and vacant lots, there is a majestic beauty in the empire that cannot be controlled or altered. The devil's breath, also known as the Santa Ana's, are seasonal winds of remembrance.

At the end of the devil's breath
Romaine Washington

July.
Wilted cereal in a bowl / we
Drown in brown milk.
The haze of sparklers and fire-
Works add to the deafening heat
That drips into

August.
Caged in by smog,
Air smells of cigarettes and black exhaust.
Surely this place is meant to
Ignite.

September.
When he arrives,
He thinks this is a flat plain,
Where desert dirt covers everything like snow
And sweat is meant for breathing.
But then –

October.
And the devil's breath laps up lotion,
Claws skin with its vicious teeth.
Yowling roofs beat whoosh and

Bend of threatened windows.
Tree leaves sound like ocean.
Stripped-dry, littered bare limbs.
The hard ones, snap - ripe for a switch.
Usedtabe gangs of tumbleweeds ran the streets;
Now solitary wadded balls of rootless limbs roll by.

November
Is a postcard miracle,
Surrounded snow cap crisp sky
Where our eyes hang glide like eagles.
We perch low in the valley shadow
Straining to see the walk of fame,
Sunset and Hollywood,
Palm Springs.
Peer into the pier of the Pacific.
Every mountain peak is
Paramount. He says
If it weren't for the devil's breath,
I'd never know where we are, and
Just how beautiful.

Keenan Norris

from *Brother and the Dancer*

*

After finally figuring out that Erycha no longer wanted him, Ricky didn't come around anymore. Instead he sent the girls he slept with to find Erycha at school, at the store, wherever, whenever, so that they could tell her about how lucky they were and how dumb a bitch she was. Erycha didn't take any of this seriously: She knew she wasn't dumb and she could care less about being a bitch as long as she wasn't the weak kind.

She plain and simple didn't take the girls as personally as she knew Rick was hoping that she would. Unlike his quotations and his suit, this was a very predictable move on his part. He was male. As young as she was, Erycha already knew that the other half of humanity had their egos wrapped around their dicks. If you denied them sexually and at the level of their ego, they would let you know about it. If these females were Rick's way of moving on she was good with that, just so long as he moved on. He had some truly annoying spiteful bitches hauling his water for him, but she was good with that, too. The girls were nothing to her. All she wanted was to be left to herself. She was best by herself.

*

It was in fall of her senior year in high school that she saw the blue dancer's dress again. It had been months since any of Ricky's girls had approached her and then one day walking home from step practice, Erycha saw the pretty little dress again. There were a million little blue dresses in the world, but somehow she just knew that the one the girl walking up Del Rosa Avenue was wearing was the exact same one that Ricky had bought for her and that she had left at his place when she broke up with him.

The girl inside the dress had a red-light, traffic-stopping figure. She overflowed and fell out of the dress in front and even more in back. Her butt was a convex table, the dress a tablecloth barely covering her. She didn't have the dancer's body that the dress seemed meant for, but she had a shapeliness that surpassed the dress. Erycha noticed the cars along Del Rosa slowing as they passed the girl and felt suddenly totally physically inadequate. It had to do with the dress, with the girl, with the fact that Erycha was dressed in sweat pants and a sweat-soaked top and her unmade hair was a wet mess and she smelled like a man and she was walking alone.

Ricky's previous females had been average at best. They were the kind of desperate girls who felt they had nothing but sex to offer. The first one was his G Street jump-off: The girl confronted Erycha outside the high school. She was about six feet tall in her heels so when she walked up to Erycha she literally talked down to her. The spiteful part was that she straight-out told Erycha how even before Erycha was out of the picture she and Ricky liked to have sex in the bed Erycha shared with her man. Then she asked Erycha if she wanted in on a threesome. The second girl stepped to Erycha in the grocery store one day. She was light-skinned, probably mixed with white or Latina, and small like Erycha. She had a mouth on her too, talking about Ricky's size and calling Erycha all kinds of bitches and heifers. They were both small but Erycha was strong and she knew it; knew she could yank the girl by her long hair and slam her into the wine rack if she made her angry enough. When she could maim her so easy, it was hard to feel anything but superior. The third female Erycha barely remembered except that the woman was a little bit older than the others, wore a weave and had what looked like a wedding ring on her finger. She spoke softly, but said most of the same messed-up things. Erycha felt sorry for her soul.

Erycha had as little respect for those females as Ricky did for them. But this girl coming up the street was a little different. More unselfconscious than the others, she walked like someone who wasn't trying to convince herself that the brother she had just slept with still wanted her.

Erycha was the nervous one now. She played her hands through her sweat-drenched hair, tried to make it magically sit up or lie down or fly sideways or anything half-respectable. But, as usual, it was impossible to make wet hair be anything respectable.

As they neared each other, the girl's eyes narrowed on Erycha. She swung her purse in a full looping circle. Erycha could tell something was about to happen. She nodded at the girl. The girl didn't nod back. Erycha kept her eyes on the little purse.

"I like them bangs," the girl offered. "An' that top, too. Gotta get me one 'a them right there." The insults came off her mouth sweet as syrup.

Erycha stopped in the middle of Del Rosa. The girl stopped, too. Erycha waited for something to come to mind, something that she could say in return. But nothing came.

"Yeah," the girl in the blue dress went on, "You don't say much, do you? Makin things all awkward, is that a strategy or somethin?"

Right then, Erycha regretted not having made friends with the younger girls on the step squad who had replaced her graduated friends Quincia and Lindsay. Now she walked home alone from practice. "I just finished step practice," she finally managed. "I'm tired." She still had her eyes on the purse.

"I have a team out in Moreno Valley. I was born an' raised in this filthy ol' town, but I got my ass to Moreno Valley. Ain't nothin worthwhile out here if you tryna put a life together. Jus my dude, he stay out here. An' family. But they all movin down my way. But, yeah, we jus won the all-Inland Empire step competition. Y'all heard bout that?"

Erycha decided from the casual way the girl was holding the purse, she had no intention to use it for a weapon. She figured she was on safe ground conversationally, too, talking about dance. "I'm not real big into steppin, it's just what I do right now. College, I'ma prob'ly do ballet or modern, somethin more technical, more artistic than step squad."

The girl gripped her crescent-shaped hips. "I don't know nothin related to all that stuff you was jus talkin. I jus know if a chick can really get it, if she can dance, she gon' be good at steppin. If she scared 'a dancin like she still black, if she jus on some white girl shit, then that chick need to sit her ass down, read some poetry or somethin. Authentic or ya never meant it, na'mean."

Erycha noticed how doughy the girl's face was, how the plumpness of her cheeks almost overwhelmed her small eyes. Her make-up sat on her face in thick, inconsistent layers. Erycha started to feel better about her undone hair and sweaty clothing. "Yeah, girl, I know what you mean. But there's more to dance than just stompin the ground an' shakin our yams. Any female with enough ass in her jeans can do that. I'm tryina dance. Dance is an art form."

The girl shrugged and had to re-adjust herself in the dress. A car riding past honked at her, or at both girls. The dress had a completely different style to it now that this thick girl was wearing it, Erycha decided. Where on Erycha's frame it would have been elegant and wearable on a dance-floor or at a cookout or to a wedding, now, on this body the dress spoke sex; sex, simple and plain. The girl could wear it all the same places, but people would see her differently than they would see a girl like Erycha. Erycha saw the girl differently than she saw herself.

"An art form," the girl repeated. "Art form. Like I said, poetry."

Erycha had lived in the hood her whole life. Did you have to dance like you lived? She wanted to say No. There were all kinds of recently immi-grated Mexicans and Guatemalans and whatnot right in the depths of the hood who wouldn't know stepping from the Virgin of Guadalupe. There were folks in the hood who couldn't dance at all, let alone bust down. Some of them were even big-hipped black women who didn't hardly have to do anything but wind themselves around a little bit to get men want-ing to give them the good news and still they couldn't even manage that. She went on and on, talking about all these exceptions to the rule. She didn't even speak on the classical colored folk who were into ballet, which was probably only Erycha herself, but, shit, she counted for something too, even if she knew deep down that right now she was mostly into ballet as an argument: Something she could bring up out of the darkness to show her difference, her divine spark; but truth be known, she didn't have a studio to practice at and hadn't performed in she couldn't remember how long, for more reasons than she cared to recall. Did you have to dance like you lived? She wanted to say No.

She could see the girl's mind working, trying to come up with some way to come back at her now. The purse swung out in another big, looping, absent-minded motion. Then she did what Erycha did not expect her to do: She conceded.

"Whatever, girl. Go ballet ya'self to death. I could give a damn. I gotta go tend to my grandmamma, pay my granddaughter dues. Cain't keep forgettin to visit the family house. By the way, Ricky movin to Mo Val." With that, the girl brushed past Erycha, and started up Del Rosa's long slow incline.

Erycha didn't care where Ricky went to. But she still watched his new girl stroll off because it was too hard not to. That switching slow nowhere to go way her whole body moved when she walked, the way she held her purse like a chain link, letting it wave back and forth in those wide careless loops. Her dress was working overtime now to keep her inside of it. Erycha half-expected some skanky old man draped in furs to drive up next to her and try and pimp her on the spot. But that didn't happen. The girl just walked and walked in the hot afternoon sun, ignoring the honking horns and the money waved from the windows of cars that slowed as they neared her and the heat of the day. When she had finally disappeared into the gray-white afternoon light, Erycha turned around and made the same demeaning journey going the other way.

San Bernardino Swap Meet Series

Thomas McGovern

SAN BERNARDINO, SINGING

SAN BERNARDINO, SINGING

The Wash
Gayle Brandeis

"Let's get married," Mason said as he was driving us down Baseline to Goldman's Medical Supply. "I mean it, Shelby."

"Keep your eye on the road," I told him. He was looking right at my face.

"No, really, Shelby. I mean it. What do you say we get married?"

"Mason, you're not even my boyfriend." I slurped up the last of my white cherry Icee.

"That's okay," said Mason. There was a funny shine in his eyes. "People do it all the time. We like each other, right?"

"Of course we do, Mason," I said, but by then we had pulled up in front of Goldman's and I squeezed one last drop through the red straw with the little spoon on the end and we had other things to think about.

Mason needed surgical tubing. He and some friends were going to play war games out in the wash the next day. Surgical tubing made the best sling shots for water balloons. The wash is out by the foot of the San Bernardino Mountains. It is probably a dry river bed, full of rocks, all the water washed away. It would be a rock lover's dream, except all the rocks look the same—white. Maybe they look different to rock lovers.

The smell at Goldman's gives me the creeps—it's like vinegar and old people and the tape on the bottom of maxi pads all mixed together. While Mason tested out surgical tubing—what stretches farther, what springs back faster—I looked around. Usually when I go into a store I can find at least one thing I'd be happy to bring home, but not there. No bed pans or oxygen machines for me, thank you. Goldman's has a whole section of prosthetics—fake arms, eyes, breasts, feet. It must feel weird to have a glass eye in your head, like a permanent brain freeze. I guess I wouldn't mind slipping some fake boobs into my bra, but that would be a fine how-do-you for any guy I might pick up. Take off my shirt and my boobs fall out? I don't think so.

Back in the truck, I felt kind of strange. I took some of the hundred feet of tubing out of the bag and started yanking on it. It felt good to pull it with both hands, to feel the resistance in between. All those body parts must have got to me. I felt like I was made out of something very flimsy. I looked over at Mason and said "Okay, Mason. I'll marry you."

Mason smiled and we started driving toward the mountains. We didn't talk much. I kept pulling at the tubing and wishing I could remember how to do Cat's Cradle like I did when I was a kid. I could make a hammock, a Jacob's ladder, and a spider web, all with string laced around my fingers.

Mason drove past the wash. He put on his sunglasses because the rocks were so bright. I pulled down the visor and squinted my eyes. We drove a little bit up into the foothills. Then Mason turned into a dirt parking lot. The place looked like a horse ranch. There was a wooden sign with a bride and groom tied to a pole burnt into it.

"The Hitching Post!? You've got to be kidding, Mason."

He shook his head. "You and me, we're getting ourselves hitched!" He grabbed my hand and we ran to the log-cabin style cabin, dust flying all around us, like rice.

Inside was a little lobby with a desk, some card chairs, and a revolving dessert case filled with rings and corsages. Orchids, I think, and some carnations.

A man walked into the room, eating a sandwich. There was mayonnaise on his face. "Oh, excuse me," he said. "I didn't know anyone was here."

"Here we are!" Mason said brightly.

"Well, well," the man wiped his face. Instead of wiping the mayonnaise off, he just sort of smeared it across his cheek. "You two fixing to get married?" I could swear he looked at my stomach. To see if I was pregnant, I guess. I glared at him.

"Yes, sir, we are!" I had never seen Mason that excited before. He was even bouncing up and down on his toes.

"Okay, then. I'll get you started on the formalities…" He pushed some papers our way.

"I'm keeping my last name," I told Mason.

"Fine by me, Shelby. You don't need my name." Mason wrote down his birthday.

We filled out all the papers and paid the man $55—$20 for the license, $30 for the ceremony, $5 for a Polaroid shot. We followed the man through the swinging saloon-style doors into the wedding chapel. It was a big wood room with stained glass-style stickers on the windows. There were about 10 rows of split log pews. A woman sat in the front row. She was very old and small, with a lavender chiffon dress and house slippers with holes so big, you could see a couple of toes.

The man went behind the podium and put his sandwich on a shelf back there. He wore a red plaid shirt, a bolo tie with a cactus closing it, dark blue jeans with a big belt buckle, and cowboy boots. He wiped his hands on his jeans. "Reverend Thomas." He reached his palm out to Mason. He didn't even look at me, or my stomach, again.

I don't remember much about the getting married part, what was said and everything. I do remember the lady in the front row was crying. I remember thinking "Why should she be crying? I'm wearing sweat pants, for Pete's sake!" I also remember the ring. Mason pulled it out of his pocket, one of those candy ones, with a green plastic ring and a huge purple candy diamond on top. It was dusted with pocket lint. It barely fit on my finger.

I sort of panicked when it was time for him to kiss the bride. I had never kissed Mason before, and maybe now I even had to sleep with him. We were going to be husband and wife, after all. But Mason just kissed me French style, a peck on each cheek. His breath smelled like a radio, charged and hot.

Later, we stopped at Rosa Maria's, where the burritos are so big, it feels like you're holding a baby in a tortilla. Being married didn't feel much different. I don't know what I was expecting to change. The only thing that was different was how aware of Mason's body I was, since I was probably going to have to have sex with him, and I never even thought of him that way before, at least not that I would admit to myself. He had a big body—not fat, but big. His hands were big, too. Kind of like a bear.

Mason drove me home. He opened the car door for me, gave me a hug and kissed my forehead. "Good night, wife," he said.

"Good night, Mason," I said back to him, and walked to my apartment by myself, Being married wasn't so bad, I decided.

The next day, Mason and his friends took their surgical tubing and went out to play war games at the wash. Mason's friend, Alan, one of his very best buddies, had this brilliant idea. He decided to launch a rock instead of a water balloon. Just as a joke. It was a small rock, but it hit Mason square in the temple. Turned me into a widow, just like that.

Someone called 911 from their truck, and people came to take Mason away in an ambulance, covered by a sheet. Alan left in a patrol car, screaming his heart out from all eye-witness accounts. Mason's room mate, Kevin, called to tell me about it. He knew Mason and I were close. He didn't know we were married, but he knew we were close.

When I got to Mason's place near Cal State, I realized all of Mason's stuff was probably mine by law. There wasn't much I wanted, but I could take anything, and it would be okay. I could have his truck. Maybe he even had life insurance. I could leave San Bernardino, get a condo in Palm Desert with life insurance. But then people might think I was some sort of Black Widow—marry a guy, he dies the next day, she gets all the stuff. Pretty fishy, even to me.

"Do you think it would be okay if I took some of Mason's CDs?" I asked Kevin. I decided not to say anything about us getting married.

"Go ahead." Kevin ran his fingers through his hair. He was still in pajama pants, but it looked like he hadn't slept in days, or like he had slept too much. "He'd want you to have them. Take whatever you want. His mother's sure as hell not going to want this crap."

I went into Mason's bedroom. His bed—a mattress on the ground—was unmade. I sat down on it. On a milk crate next to the bed was the Polaroid from our wedding. Three things caught the light in that picture—the streak of mayonnaise on the Reverend's face, the tears in our witness' eyes, and Mason's smile. The flash had turned my eyes red.

I looked at the picture and all of a sudden it hit me. Mason was dead. He was really, truly, dead, and I never even kissed him on the lips. When I started crying, the tears were big and hot. They fell on my candy ring, rinsing the lint off, making the purple shine like a real-life diamond before the sugar started to slowly melt away.

The Match, the Leaf, the Soaring Spirit
Kathleen Alcalá

At first, you think you imagined it - a little flicker out the side of your eye, the pattern of leaves moving in the breeze, casting a shadow onto the worn linoleum floor.

But then, the distinct smell, sharp in the front of your nose, of something burning.

Finally, the crackling sound of something surrendering, being utterly, hopelessly consumed by the flames. And it is glorious, a ritual, a prayer, an offering on the altar of the badly swept floor to the wild gods of chance, those cruel little men who never gave her a chance.

She always denied it. Of course she did. No one ever saw her start one, noticed the missing matches or the scraps of paper in her pockets. They were nothing. Like her life that had amounted to nothing except a handful of piano students, a few musty books that once belonged to her father, and a couple of drab second-hand dresses.

She had been pretty when she was young. High cheekbones, hair that turned reddish in the sun. She and her sisters used to do each other's hair. They were always together, but after she went walking just that one time with Enrique, her mother had taken her to the doctor, just to make sure.

She almost died of embarrassment, a good way to guarantee she would never show her secrets to a man again.

But, oh, that afternoon. They sat on the grass and laughed. He told her stories about the world, the sea, places he had been stationed in the Navy. He told her stories she barely understood. At first she laughed to be polite, but then she laughed to feel it inside her lungs and mouth. It was like swallowing a soap bubble, making her giddy and light. He lit a cigarette, cupping his hands around the flame to protect it from the wind. He blew his breath in long streams that faded away before his face. What did he look like? His face had faded, too. Afterwards, he let her hold the lighter, flick the wheel that made the spark. She felt different that day, more alive, as though a veil had been pulled back that usually kept her from hearing and seeing so much around her. The grass had been warm and prickly, and boys were playing catch with a baseball, heckling each other in Spanish.

First came the early, flickering part, which she often stopped before it amounted to anything, then came the smell, and finally the sound. If she heard someone coming, she could swiftly step on it, pretend to be sweeping with a broom worn to a nub, whatever she had been set to do in the first place.

"Ignacia, what are you doing?" the señora might ask in a low, accusing voice, drawing out the 'naaa' of her name.

Ignacia would feel her face go red, a terrible giveaway even when she had not done anything. "Nothing." She kept her eyes cast down. "Just sweeping, like you told me." She was nothing. She was a leaf in the wind, scattered like the leaves before her in the neglected patio. There was something she was trying to remember. She tried to hold an empty space in her mind, in her gaze, to mask the thoughts that scurried madly around and around in her head. But something always leaked out of her face that they did not like, or that scared them.

Each time, the señora would eventually tire of keeping such a close eye on her. She needed the room for another child, a grandchild, a sewing room. Once, Ignacia heard a señora say to her brother, she needed the money, but why keep someone there who had to be watched constantly? She belonged in a Home. She watched, half-hidden in the doorway, as her brother gave the woman some more cash. Without being told, Ignacia gathered her few belongings to move again.

The first time really had been an accident. While sweeping the kitchen floor, she had impulsively picked up some onionskins and placed them on the stove.

Later, she saw how they caught fire and burned when she heated some soup. Such a lovely color. Such a nasty smell. Fidelia came in and yelled at her, asked what she was doing. The flame flared briefly, out of control for just a moment, made her heart leap. She hadn't done anything wrong since walking with Enrique without telling anyone, so many years ago. He had looked at her in a way no one ever had before, while they were sitting on the grass. He had placed his hand over hers, and she did not pull away. What would happen to her once Fidelia was gone? Every day her sister grew more frail, never able to completely catch her breath. She clutched at her chest. Her lips, more often than not, were blue.

She and her sister Fidelia had lived in the old family house for years, but upon Fidelia's death, her brother Luis and sister Beca sold the house for the money. It was to support her, they said. But they had lived for years and years without selling the house, so she did not understand why now. Ignacia had since moved more times than she could remember. Could it be more times than her family had moved during the Depression? No matter how much her brother offered to pay, after a month or five or six, Ignacia moved on. She was quiet, submissive, and devout. She was personally clean, if a bit messy. She kept scraps of paper. She said it was so she could remember things, but what did she have to remember? It was that last part that got her in trouble.

No one else wanted Ignacia, especially not her brother's wife, who kept her gaudy house just so, bright red carpet and velvet couches. There were tassels on the curtains in her kitchen. Ignacia wanted to tear them off, put them in the sink. They would probably burn nicely, sending up a horrible smell. Maybe his wife could see it in Ignacia's eyes, her desire to see it all go up in flames.

The best time came when her sister Beca took them out to their house, then left them alone while the family went to the grocery store for ice cream.

"Don't touch this light switch," Beca said, pointing at a switch on the wall. "There's something wrong with it. We have to get it fixed."

Why did they all go? Why did they leave her alone with Fidelia? They must have known what she would do.

As soon as the car pulled away and Fidelia went to the bathroom, Ignacia flicked the switch. At first, nothing happened. She could hear a buzzing sound. Then an odd smell began to build, somewhere between lightning and old clothes. Fidelia returned just in time to witness a bolt of electricity escape the ceiling light and plunge into the floor, where it danced in a perfect ring of yellow and blue flame. She looked at Ignacia and called 911.

By the time the family returned, the fire department already had the fire out. They watched in dismay as the bulky firemen packed up their gear and filed out, leaving them with a perfectly round hole burnt in the carpet. The fire had been small enough to contain with a hand-held extinguisher. Ignacia learned later that it smelled bad for weeks. Her only regret was that the firehouse was only two blocks away. The fire truck arrived within minutes. Imagine the glorious sight if the house had been engulfed in flames, the thick smoke rising above the busy street, and rubberneckers jostling to see if there were deaths, to see who could do such a thing.

Maybe they would have called the police, taken her away in handcuffs, the way she imagined Enrique had been taken away. She wondered if they took his cigarette lighter from him. The police questioned him, but there was nothing conclusive. Ignacia had been of age to consent, if barely, and Enrique admitted nothing. The family did not press charges. It would only cause more of a scandal. The sooner it could be forgotten, the better. Ignacia was kept home after that, and did not finish school, although once she had been the best speller in her class, even in English.

Ignacia would not talk about any of it. Fidelia gave up, assumed that both of them would end their lives in a painful conflagration. But her heart and lungs failed first, and Ignacia began her life as a nomad. In some ways, it reminded her of her childhood - the cardboard box that she sat in and was hers alone until she was four, only leaving it to get food or collect another book. Now, she carried her meager box of things to place under the next narrow bed, next to her "good" pair of shoes, slightly less run down, in case she had a chance to go to church. Once, seeing the old chanclas Ignacia was wearing for shoes, Beca's daughter had stepped out of her own shoes and let Ignacia try them on. They had fit, and she let her keep them, running back to the car barefoot on the scorching pavement.

All the church-goers of her younger years were gone now, the gossipers who saw her with Enrique that day and told her mother. Only Ignacia and her brother and sister Beca were left. Beca never took her to the house again, only visiting in whatever spare bedroom became her temporary home. Sometimes she put up a picture of her parents, the two of them standing stoically, enduring the hot sun while the photographer took his time. She still remembered the hat her mother wore in the photo, turned down at either corner like a sad clown mouth.

Ignacia barely remembered Enrique. She had not known him outside of church, but he came up and talked to her one day after services, asked her to meet him at the park. Ignacia does not know where her mother was that afternoon, why she wasn't watching, probably busy with her younger brother or sister. She doesn't really remember what happened, if anything. Only her mother asking a lot of things she didn't understand afterwards, about her clothes and her body, to remember that her body was the temple of the Holy Spirit, and not to lie. What did he do? She didn't know, and the doctor said there was 'no evidence' of tampering. It didn't matter. Ignacia's reputation was ruined, her mother said. She never saw Enrique again.

What if she had married him instead, had lived in a big house and had children? She tried, sometimes, to imagine them around a dining room table, saying grace, Enrique with his shiny black hair, a pack of cigarettes and his lighter on the table next to his plate. Would he smoke around the children? She had more trouble imagining children. Maybe he would tell them stories, make them laugh. Be kind to them. But they would have to do something to have children, to make her embarazada, something her mind shied away from. Something her mother had never exactly said, but that it only happened to married people or sinvergüenzas - shameless women. She could still hear the word in her mother's voice, shaming her, making her eyes sting even now.

It was better this way, alone. Except he had let her hold his cigarette lighter, a shiny gunmetal blue, something she would never be allowed to do now. Her brother made it clear to each new señora, who were all beginning to run together now. If their husbands smoked, the lighters and matches had to be hidden away from her.

Ignacia was trying to remember something, but what was it? She wondered how this life would end. Would she expire in a pillar of fire, Joan of Arc to her mother's iron rules? Or in a tepid puff of smoke one afternoon when her landlady was out? Would she become an angel, or was she condemned to eternal flame for not telling her mother that she was going walking with Enrique? Would she join her parents and Fidelia in Heaven, and what would that be like anyway? She hoped that it would smell like burning leaves.

Ignacia wondered if she would have a box in which to keep her things - the little book of psalms a kind American lady gave her, the print too tiny to read, a crocheted doily in red and orange, some photos of people she once knew: Her friend Gloria, Tuti with her husband, Cordelia with a foot on the running board of her car. They looked happy, stuck in those little photos, always in the same clothes, the same smiles on their faces. They must all be dead by now, devoured by the flames of time.

She did not know. She prayed to God for forgiveness, and stuffed another scrap of paper into her sweater pocket, the one with the handful of dried leaves. There was something she had scribbled on the paper, something she needed to remember. It had been different that one day in the park, almost like being free. Had she tried to write to Enrique? Once, years later, Fidelia said he had sent a letter, but their mother kept it, threw it away. Basura, she had said. Trash.

She loved her own skin. Stroking it, smoothing lotion into it. The way it turned a golden brown in the sun, never burning. People admired her skin, her face, told her how lovely it was. She looked down and said thank you, the way she finally learned to take a compliment, rather than protesting in the Mexican way.

She tried not to be vain, but secretly, she was. When she was twelve, she realized that she was going to be beautiful. Her long hair enveloped her shoulders when she walked, billowed about her skinny frame that was on the verge of womanhood. Staring at herself in the mirror, Roma would not answer her mother, preferring her own company to the constantly blaring television.

In her head, stories played, better stories than those her parents watched. In her stories, people flew. They visited other planets where gravity could be adjusted as they wanted - a light day when there was much work to be done, a heavy day when all they did was sit around and read magazines.

Roma's clothes were mostly hand-me-downs, but she begged her mother for a sewing machine and took everything in. She pegged her sister's jeans, put rick-rack around the hems, and made skirts she could shorten just by pulling them up around her waist, hidden by her t-shirts.

It was the era of go-go boots, and most girls wore the white ones. Roma wore heavy dark boots, the kind Julie Christie would have worn in Dr. Zhivago. No matter that it was sunny and 75 in the winter.

She woke up sighing. "Roma, what are you thinking?" asked her mother. She could not say. She could not say that she was in the arms of not one man, but two, and it was a heavy day. They planned to spend all day in bed having sex and reading magazines. Instead, Roma got up and got ready for school, keeping her dreams to herself.

At fourteen, a boy walked her home from school. He was a year or two older, and his name was Chris. Roma was embarrassed, but what could she do? He walked her home one other time, before he realized that her family would not let him into the house, much less let her go out with him. Not then, maybe never. Not because he was too old, or she was too young, but because he was Anglo. His tall frame, the sort that would run to fat at the other end of his life, stood out in their neighborhood. It was never a good idea to stand out in this neighborhood, close to the high school, close to the west side.

Instead, her father invited boys from the school where he taught over to the house. He asked his daughter to serve them cold soda. She did as he asked, but only because the boys let her choose to watch anything she wanted on television. They liked the same television that she did. Star Trek, The Man From U.N.C.L.E. These programs baffled her parents, who preferred the television shows where people were laughing somewhere all the time. They believed every single thing that Walter Cronkite said, and Roma did, too. Except the part about walking on the moon. Roma's mother did not believe that, because how would they get there? It was too far, it was in Heaven, with God and Jesus and the angels.

Roma read her school assignments, but barely completed her written homework. It was so repetitive. Someone passed her a note in the middle of English Composition one day. "Where can I get birth control?" How was she to know? Roma turned around. It was Nancy, a white girl in the class. Why was she asking Roma? Because they thought she was smart, that she would have that answer, too. The teacher demanded to see the note. Half the class had already read it, and hooted in anticipation of Roma getting into trouble. Instead, she swallowed it. This made her popular for at least a week.

Roma dreamed. She read books she checked out of the library. She wanted to visit another planet. She wanted to sleep with the entire cast of Star Trek. The boys her father brought home were mama's boys, being groomed to be the first in their families to go to college. All they had to do was not get killed in high school. No one asked Roma what she wanted to do when she graduated. Her sisters were nurses, both working at St. Bernardine's, both living at home, waiting to get married. They brought back stories about the emergency room cases, the gunshots, the rapes, the baby born to someone who was both a man and a woman. They would whisper these stories to their mother so that Roma only half heard them. Her mother would clasp her hand over her mouth as though she had been the one to say these things, but she could not get enough. To her, these stories proved that if you stayed home at night, locked the door and watched television, no one would bother you. Roma spent hours listening to music, staring at the mirror, the only other human being who would meet her gaze.

On Sundays, they sometimes drove to see their relatives in Los Angeles. It was a long drive, and her father did not like to use his day off to do it, but he had no choice. All the relatives were on her mother's side, and all his lived in Mexico. When they would go to see her aunts Ignacia and Fidelia, Roma wondered at their lives, what they had done to end up as solteras, old maids. Hadn't any boys walked them home? They were never allowed to be alone when they were growing up, her mother said. The sisters always had to be with each other if they went out. Roma's parents had never been alone together before they married.

Her aunts had never kissed a man, Roma realized. They never held a man in their arms, or felt that hot surge of blood in their bodies. Ignacia would squint at the sun as if she never went outside, except when they came to visit. They brought food that did not need to be cooked, fruit and cans of tuna, cookies and crackers. Roma knew that Ignacia was not supposed to be around matches, that fires seemed to just start around her.

"Have you heard of spontaneous combustion?" Roma asked one day. Fidelia told her to mind her own business, that she was rude. It was hard to have a conversation with her aunts. She wondered how old they were.

Roma looked down one day at Ignacia's shoes, and saw that they were men's house slippers, brown corduroy worn as though someone had walked a long way in them. She stepped out of her shoes, practical flats, but cute. "Here," she said. "Try these." Ignacia struggled out of her slippers and into the shoes. Suddenly she looked better, taller. She was already tall and thin, but she smiled as she stood up straight, and Roma recognized her own ghost, the girl in the mirror grown old. She was missing a few teeth. The shoes fit just right.

"Cinderella," said Roma. "Keep them." Ignacia just kept smiling, not even hiding her bad teeth the way she usually did.

"Don't you like them anymore?" asked her mother.

"Yes, but look how well they fit her. Look at the shoes she's been wearing."

Her mother started to say something, but stopped. Fidelia looked exasperated, muttered something under her breath and walked away. Her shoes were not great, but they were better than Ignacia's old slippers.

Roma really liked those shoes, but she knew that she would escape. Maybe she would not travel to another planet, although she really wanted to, more than anything, but she would at least live in a different place, and spend time with people she was not related to, people of her own choosing. She would meet boys who were not mama's boys, who would read books they didn't have to read. She would know the answer to Nancy's question.

Ignacia, Roma knew, would never escape, not in this world. Someone would always be watching for that flickering light, that haunted look in Ignacia's eyes. Roma would have to escape for both of them.

Ignacia had not been sleeping well at this house. She got mixed up, not remembering that Fidelia was gone now, and would not return. Wondering when her brother would visit again. She liked these shoes, but did not remember where they came from. The bed had squeaky springs, and groaned every time she turned over on the thin mattress, waking her. She had to remember to tell him. Ignacia pulled the paper back out and tried to read her own shaky handwriting. Oh yes, she remembered now.

Every house has matches somewhere.

Kick Down Their Doors

Sheela Sitaram Free

It's the war of the home invaders
In San Bernardino: the smash-and-grab posse.
Kick down *their* doors,
in their swank gated homes
get a few *homies* together, not hard to do,
(they're letting us out every day too),
as our ghettos and barrios
went to hell a long long time ago.
so now it's time *theirs* went to hell and back too
spread the pain, the loot, the fear,
the thin icy line of hate, of stuffed up anger
that can't be snuffed out
with the cigarette butts, the mcnuggets,
the tecates-the *"pink slime"* of our lives.
Lord knows we've tried,
tried now, tried last year when we got homeless,
laid off and all, ten years ago too,
the only stories *we're* raised on.

Kick down *their* doors,
they got it all bro, we ain't,
what's the difference, you ask?
Ohhhhhhhh.
Here, no blood reds or blues
no dogs barking without HOA approval first,

just more and more fancy stuff,
HD flat screens, smart phones, laptops,
3 cars in the garage, big glass doors and windows
for everyone to see into,
so the light they love so much pours through,
the orange sunsets glow through,
making it so easy for us to see
the swap meet $50/- bucks a pop stuff,
smash and grab, in and out in 2 minutes,
laughing all the way to and from
the cool racket we've cooked up all the way from Victorville
to Rialto, Fontana, and Highland, in our posses, our crews;
the glass still shattering, shivering
as they make their way home,
as we make our quick getaway.

So we'll kick *their* doors down
As the icy fear grips them in their wallets
their impotent town hall meetings
as their rage mingles with ours
till *they* get the ghetto, the barrio,
the newly homeless,
everyone just one paycheck from being that anyway,
sitting ducks with bulls eye on our backs,
till they trade in for guns their baseball bats to beat us back with.
They should be scared, like us; we're terrified, all the time.
We're all rolling in this crap together
helpless, powerless, clueless
kicking doors down

as we can't, we won't do anything else.

We weren't always like this, you know,
goaded into nipping at your homes,
detectives, teachers, nurses, old ladies,
we really weren't,
we really weren't ever the 99%,
forget the 1%
as we go from broke to broken,
trading in our "pink slime"
for the "green slime"
choking us all in this shattered mess,
they nip at you, we nip at you,
just the way it works out here,
we're here, there, everywhere
now, sharp as ever
to kick down *your* doors.
It is the war of the home invaders.

San Bernardino Passion
Sheela Sitaram Free

Bite into the slushy passion of the persimmon out here

And sink into the orange membranous skies of San Bernardino

Its fully barbecued forest fires, its chocolatey mudslides.

When its skin is taut and ready to go

Ooooooooo eeeeeeee Ooooooo eeeee

It's persimmon passion alright,

Bite into San Bernardino and it will bite back.

Uvulaic Rhapsody

Sheela Sitaram Free

The Santa Ana
Banshees by.
The double paned glass windows
Shudder to the brink of cracking
Then stiffen up
Double barred
Secured
Locked down.
In Barstow Norco Devore.
By dawn
By dusk
The brown grey ash
Crucibled to perfection
Filters in
Eerily
Into the frills of every dainty pillow
Scrunches
The bubbles of semen hocked mattresses
For life.
The follicles are rooted by it
Crunchies bead on the tongue
Dust bowls
Pocket the back of the throat

No chilled Tecate can irrigate.
Dirt devil all you want.
In the Cajon Pass
This giant uvulaic rhapsody
Goes on.

The City Next Door
Michelle Gonzalez

As I leave Riverside,
I drive along the 215 freeway
towards San Bernardino.
It's the city where my parents met
at the Norton Force Base.
I pass the original McDonald's
where they shared fries and a shake.
The building has become a museum since then.
I then pass the semi-abandoned mall
that once had a great carousel.
We would eat at the buffet
in the mall on the weekends.

I also pass Baseline Street
which leads to Baseline Burgers.
We would have breakfast
with my grandfather after church
at St Anthony's on Western Ave.

Leaving the downtown area,
we head to the mountains
to play in the snow.

I wonder how many people

Michelle Gonzalez

pass through the city,
only knowing the violence
that they see and hear
on the television.

B.I. in the I.E.
(Dedicated to the Brandin' Iron, San Bernardino, CA)
Nan Friedley

been here since '69
was a bowling alley before that
same puckered wooden floor
ten-pin lanes
replaced by a country stage
for rising young nashville stars
fireball fridays
jack daniel's saturday
my night
thirsty thursday
no cover before 7
cheap beer till close
sat with a table of friends
on bar stools
under the BI neon sign
learned how to dance
in a line, boot scootin' boogie
with a partner, cowboy cha-cha
dressed as a cowgirl
tight levis, justin boots
too many bud lights
cultivated courage
to try the mechanical bull
three seconds
i'll never get back again

Slow Down on Antelope Highway
Wil Clarke

Fritz Martinsen was a very dear friend of mine and fellow missionary at Ikizu in Tanzania, Africa, in the late 1960s. After he retired he was hired as a part time pastor for a church in Mojave, CA. While serving there in the 1990s, cancer caught up with him and killed him.

To get to his funeral we drove up the Cajon Pass out of San Bernardino and along the mountainous Antelope Highway through Lancaster. In the 1990s it was two-lane highway that climbed steadily up into the High Desert along the San Gabriel Mountains.

Ahead of us was a small pickup pulling a big trailer. The trailer obviously slowed him down so that he had a long line of cars following. I was immediately behind him and chafing to get around him. I looked forward to the next passing lane where we could surely pass him. But that was not to be. Selfishly, the driver did not pull over and let us pass him as the highway design suggested. Instead he just hogged the main lane.

I sputtered and fumed and questioned the driver's ancestry. My Dad, who had also known Fritz, was riding with me. He said nothing, just muttered his feelings under his breath. Eventually we reached another passing lane. This time I got around him, on the right. I heard Dad heave a sigh of relief. I was indeed angry and plotting vengeance. After I got around him and we were again on the two-lane road, I slowed down gradually to about 20 miles per hour. The selfish driver came right up to my rear bumper but then had to slow down, too.

Dad said softly and sympathetically, "Don't slow down; he may not be able to get up to speed again."

I grunted, "Serves him right!" Then I went on up the long mountain pass at normal speed leaving him far behind. I felt justified in slowing him down, but my actions bothered me. By yielding to my anger I violated the Golden Rule, furthermore I broke my own standards. Although the road hog was obviously insensitive and deserved a wakeup call, I didn't have to live with him. I do have to live with myself.

Journey to San Bernardino
Sylvia J. Clarke

By the time our bus arrived in San Bernardino, I needed toothpicks to hold my eyes open. Here's why: Three days earlier our family (Wil, Esther, Julia, Fred, and I) left Massachusetts with friends, Sam and Monda, and their children in a van—13 of us heading to New Mexico over the Christmas holidays. It worked like this: With one extra man to help with the driving, we mothers were not required to take a turn. But we had enough to keep us busy.

Monda and I periodically passed around snacks and drinks while shepherding eight children, most of them lounging, playing, or sleeping on a mattress in the back of the van. We also herded all of them to and from filling station restrooms. Day or night, every time we stopped for fuel someone shouted, "Everybody out to the bathroom!" And we all obeyed.

Routing out the sleepers or slow ones, Monda and I supervised the children as they yawned or complained, waiting their turn at the porcelain throne. When we got back into the van, it was our duty to count heads so none were left behind. We started out from Massachusetts on a Saturday night and arrived at Sam's parent's home in Farmington, New Mexico, in slightly less than 48 hours.

In the Farmington home, our family sat and fought off sleep so we would be polite guests. Someone looked up the schedule for a bus heading to southern California, our destination. In less than an hour Sam whisked us off to the bus station, and after making sure our luggage was loaded, we all boarded and headed to San Bernardino, California. There Wil's dad would meet us.

How well do you sleep sitting up in a moving vehicle? What about after three days of trying? Now you know why I have only a few memory scraps of my first time in San Bernardino. They boil down to these: warmth of a winter sun as we alighted, Dad and Mom Helen greeting us, signs along the highway for old Route 66, silhouettes of buildings against a late afternoon sun as we drove west, and hazy mountains to the right behind the city. Tiredness blotted out the rest. Only later would I begin to really experience the city called San Bernardino.

That San Bernardino Guy
Rose Baldwin

It was many years ago that I was so in love
but he's the man who on this day I am thinking of
I remember how he smelled, and his spasms when he came
but you know for the life of me I can't think of his name
I remember he was funny, and laughed at my jokes too
smart and sweet he liked to talk, and spin a tale or two
he turned a lot of heads with his hair so thick and wavy
even though all that is clear, his name? well, that escapes me
We ate at the Castaways and danced at the D I
by day we hiked on mountains, at night we searched the sky
how did I let him get away? this beautiful heart throb
I'd look for him on Google if, wait, was his name Bob?
I thought we'd love forever and share happiness galore
with slights and hurts we grew apart until we spoke no more
at the end I felt carved out, my heart wounded and lame
still, I sit in wonder, when I think of what's-his-name

The I-10

—San Bernardino County

Cynthia Anderson

Born in 1897, a San Bernardino native son,
my grandfather lived to be 100. Late in life,
when we would take him out for a drive,
he would point to some shopping mall
off the I-10 and say,
We used to hunt rabbits there.

When he retired from title insurance,
he farmed in Cherry Valley, fruit trees
and eggs. Later, in Yucaipa, he cared for
my grandmother, who lingered two decades
after a crippling stroke—with a will to live
she learned as a child in Randsburg,
where her father worked for the mines.

Time and again, I would head down the coast,
pick up the I-10 in Santa Monica, barrel straight
through L.A.'s polluted heart to the hinterlands,
find my way to the Yucaipa house by rote,
gripping the wheel as I ran the gauntlet,
breathing a sigh of relief at the exit.

Cynthia Anderson

Then Riverside, a convalescent hospital
on Magnolia Drive. My grandfather recalled
when the stately palms were planted,
Sunday drives before the first world war.
He joined my grandmother at Desert Lawn,
hardly a resting place—the I-10 a noisy witness
to the end of their lives and the world they knew.

They Know Us at the Food Pantry
Cindy Bousquet Harris

Help unload, get an extra bag:
cherry tomatoes, asparagus,
even meat – skip first Fridays,
line is out the door and down the street
like summer squash;
who knew there were so many
kinds of bok choy?
Geometry of chips, crackers,
more than could be used in a misnamed
foreseeable future;
soup and peaches, pinto beans
fill our river basket,
just add mix to avocados –
be sure to peel the skin.
Wish-hollow peppers, red or yellow,
ginger snaps
still taste the same
from dented boxes,
strawberry yogurt not quite expired;
you can eat the carrots
with your skin on.

San Bernardino
Alexis Gonzalez

When asked the question
"Where are you from,"
And I say
"San Bernardino"
Should I be ashamed?
Should I brace
For a sad face?
Should I just not say
the name
of the place
known for terrorists,
known for hate?
Should I try to explain
That news coverage
Doesn't disclose the bigger
Parts of this city
That don't consist of tragedy?
This city is not just
What's seen on a screen.
It is not just
Pictures on T.V.

San Bernardino Hood
Robert Porter

San Bernardino is beautiful in so many great ways.
Just take the dogs wandering, and learning you may.
Wind through the trees, with the rattling leaves.
An energy so deep that you have to truly believe.
Cooper's hawk swishing, through the dry hot air.
Scatter go the pigeons, as they escape their despair.
Crunch of the flowers, then kicking the stray sticks.
Sound of the freeway, and the peeps of the chicks.
Growl of the bad dog, better be a good tempered pup.
A crackle of the leaf litter, as the lizard says what's up?
See life is what you make it and if you tend to choose good.
A star you will become, three puffs of smoke from the hood.

Rory Murray

Wig Wam

Living Mural West Wall

Easter Morning
Micah Chatterton

I try to tell myself this place belongs
to everyone, not just the quiet families
looking to make church in dry riverbeds
and groves of thirst-split oaks,
not just a pair of greying hippies flopped
on a white boulder, or a son on shoulders
driving his father-shaped horse by the hair,
or his mother silently slipping ahead
to hide plastic eggs by the trailside.
But, Christ, somebody's radio back
at the trailhead keeps getting louder
the farther we walk up the valley wall,
a Spanish station cranked high enough
to muffle the grump of an old generator,
trumpet lines and guitar licks slapping
every stone, acorn, threadbare blackberry,
child and hiker for miles around.
Roasted peanuts and blackened corn husks,
the bitterer smells of a large gathering,
a reunion maybe, echo off the tree trunks.
We came here to be alone, or feel alone
at least, surrounded by what God made,
but now there's music everywhere, warbling
choruses I can't quite catch, meditate away
or stop myself from resenting, from looking

back at each treebreak for a quick glimpse
of whoever thought to bring a PA system
to the National Forest on a Sunday morning.
Turning a bend, Samuel tugs my chin
toward a blue egg Jenny stashed
in the withering shade under a fern.
'Nuther blue one, he calls. She grins,
pretending to be amazed that he could spot
such a well-hidden jewel. I toddle down,
suddenly aware of how much heavier
he's become lately, and hand Sam the egg.
In one bell-half of the plastic shell he finds
a lozenge of clear, smooth quartz, in the other
a pine cone the size of a pinky nail.
He holds them both in front of my eyes,
squealing, until I stumble on a root and realize
the radio cut out some moments ago.
Like nothing, Samuel drops the stone
and crumbles the pine cone between
his thumb and finger. *Again, again,*
he says, his voice still babyish, asking only
to find whatever's precious in this place,
not to carry or keep it as his own.
I hear girls laughing back by the river, clanging
pots and bottles, guttering through the wash,
singing. *Otra vez, otra vez,* maybe.

Sphinx
Micah Chatterton

1

When I was young
I gave a tangerine to a baby
to see what would happen.
At first, his mouth an unwound flower
of thin lips and throbbing gums,
he gnawed its curves for hours, savoring
the chill, the smooth of the skin, the fleshy
give, the sugared cells bursting inside.
Each day I pulled another fruit
from my pocket for him to teeth on, to slather,
to press against the stigma of his tongue
until he knew the scent, shape, and color
of a tangerine across a room,
and would leap angrily from my hip
whenever we passed the produce aisle.
Once, barely, a tooth broke in the night.
The next morning, mouthing a beautiful
mandarin, he tore the rind to the bitter white.
He screamed, of course, lips pulled in,
eyes wet, but bit again, then again, waiting
for the flash of sour, for the invisible
sliver of glass always aching to remind
us it was something else once.

2

A man and a woman become
a husband and a wife,
almost without realizing.
Every week he brings her a bag of fat
tangerines from a shack in the groves
by the veteran's cemetery.
Across the dinner table, he hands
her a mesh sack stretched wide
by gorgeous orange globes,
each bearing a winter's worth
of sunlight inside.
I love them,
she giggles.
I love the way
they spray sweetness
into my mouth
when I bite hard
with my front teeth.
I love the way
the segments look like ears,
tiny little babies' ears
I can eat,
she says.
He draws a knuckle
lightly along the moon edge
of the back of her arm.

You know that's how
cannibals talk,
right?

3

Somewhere, a magpie
caught the quick green glint of a knife blade,
even in all that snow.
I pulled three tangerines from the belly
of my pack and laid them in a sunbeam.
Somewhere, a black bear
never got cold or hungry enough to sleep,
a dazed beggar, wandering river to road.
She took one and he took one. I pierced
the bottom hollows with a soured fingertip.
Somewhere, a white labrador
leapt out of a moving truck bed, called out
by wind, and never touched the ground again.
Legs splayed in a snowpack, unsure, he dug two fingers
under the rind, juice bleeding past his knuckles.
Somewhere, a book
was left in the grass and sleet, to be undone
by mice, to be remade into shelter and food.
Remembering does nothing for the remembered.
He tucked the torn skins in a little white tomb.
Somewhere, a mountain
pretended to care about the people and animals,
even the trees, shivering on its back.

4

After the frost in the night a strange man
walks the rows of stones ahead of me,
enskyed by the deep morning fog, placing
tangerines on the markers. He bows to each.
His grey hand metronomes quietly
to the banana box propped on his right shoulder,
then down to the flat plane of a body and name,
or names, with a small, bright fruit,
the only sun they'll get today.
Following him, watching his dew-blurred arms
tend to hungry ghosts, I pass her by again,
as I often do, as I suddenly remembered
this morning it was her birthday last week.
I wet my knees on her scrap of grass and earth.
The tangerine on the stone sits carefully away
from the unmoving rivulets of her name,
what her job was, the date, the window thrown
open at her birth to let the world in, and slid shut
to keep her body warm a little longer.
Kneeling, I pull a milk-eyed Mason jar
of vodka tonic, which she loved as much
as I hate, and a shortbread from my pocket.
I peel the tangerine into thready petals attached
at the stem, into the white-veined rays
of a star, into a stilled canvas,
Vanishing Man with Liquor, Citrus, Grave and Cookie,

and I eat, I drink,
every bitter crumb and drop,
for all the lives I've lost.

Three Drops Balanced on an Elm Leaf—a Flame-singed Tip.

Cindy Rinne

Scent of incense floated through the Gambling hall at 19 Third Street.
Asian coins clinked. Opium pipes. Ah Wing and Jim Kang washed

laundry, cooked, and were houseboys. Almost desert town and a valley
of smoke. Intruders tolerated. Then lower wages as California crashed

in 1875. Believed earnings sent to China hurt San Bernardino's economy.
Ah, Jim, and others forced to move outside the city limits. Third Street

between Arrowhead Avenue and Sierra Way became a world of ink
bottles, Chinese porcelain bowls, and traditional cures in small glass vials.

I never knew there was a Chinatown in San Bernardino. Three drops
balanced on an elm leaf—a flame-singed tip. She arrived in 1878

covered in a red and gold embroidered brocade robe. Kwan Yin,
a Buddhist goddess of healing and compassion. She refrained

from entering Nirvana to aid the displaced. *I will not reach final
liberation until all other beings have been liberated.* Bells, singing

bowls, and chants whirled. Three drops balanced on an elm leaf—
a flame-singed tip. Wong Nim became the mayor of Chinatown

and built brick buildings surrounded by groceries, chop suey
restaurants, and mercantile shops. Wong Nim created a temple home

for Kwan Yin. A place of pilgrimage. Wondered why so many people
traveled far. Chinese gardens established east of Waterman Avenue

and Base Line. Horses clopped when farmers brought their produce
to town. Waited to purchase. Three drops balanced on an elm leaf—

a flame-singed tip. I talked to a woman yesterday at Cal State. She said,
God the Father also has God the Mother. Her name is Jerusalem.

All are born of the Mother. The Spirit (Trinity) and the bride (Mother)
say, "Come!" I walked away. Three drops balanced on an elm leaf—

a flame-singed tip. Fire destroyed Chinatown in the 1920's. Kwan Yin
still resides. Three drops balanced on an elm leaf—a flame-singed tip.

SAN BERNARDINO, SINGING

The Santa Fe Whistle
James Luna

*(Note: Before 24 hour cartoon channels TV
stations only programmed cartoons between
3-5:00 p.m. weekdays.)*

2:57 p.m.
He stands in the parking lot
Of the church
Of Our Lady of Guadalupe
With his dad
Watching the usher
Dressed as a centurion
Yell at the teenager
Undressed as Jesus,
While his mom
With the rest of the Guadalupanas
Stir pots of lentils,
Fry nopales and check the capirotada
And pray there will be enough.
3:00 p.m.
Two miles away,
The whistle
At the Santa Fe yard
Howls in suspicious overtones
At the workers,

"Break's over!"
His nine year old ears
Intuit that sound
As the only time
He controls the television:
The bear in the fedora,
The Neolithic family,
The talking grey rabbit.
Each chasing, shooting,
Exploding each other
With comic immortality
Except for today,
The first Friday
After the first full moon
After the vernal equinox.
The teenager hangs his head
And everyone, including the boy
Kneels on the pavement.
His stomach growls
Because in his religion
He cannot eat
Until his savior has died.

On the Edge
Christine Chatterton

Town growing up on the edge.

The edge of the mountains. Rugged, steep, sometimes mossy green but more often burnt brown.

A great stony arrowhead on the cliffside pointing with sharp edges down.

The edge by the rivers that come clattering out of the mountains to meander to the sea.

Named for powerful men long dead: Santa Ana, Waterman, Lytle, from when water meant life.

For orchards of trees filled with fruit of sunset orange and glowing yellow and vibrant green.

Valleys with fanciful names on the mountain's edge: Forest Falls, Oak Glen, Running Springs.

Beckoning people to come out of the dry valley and into the pines, to rest on the edge of a mountain lookout.

City built up on the edge.

The edge of the freeways and houses and crowds. Sprawling malls and tall towers. Mansions on hills.

The edge of the massive metropolis which is that brash city, LA.

The small farm towns swallowed up by the crowd. The old towns still trying to be themselves.

San Bernardino, the hub of the towns, half old now, half

new. Half growing, half falling into disuse.

Change is relentless. The metropolis spreads out. Either change or develop into something brand new.

The small bungalows and neighborhoods don't fit into that new Metrovision: all houses and no yards.

The muscular hard labor jobs are gone. Steel workers, railroad workers, builders and growers and soldiers are gone.

New jobs come slowly, but slowly they do come. Warehouses, offices, truckers and jobs fit for the edge.

People living on the edge.

Good people, strong people who have weathered the change. Neighbors together 20, 30 years or more.

Seeking the peace that retirement should bring, but finding old things lonely or no longer there.

Old churches of grand beauty now only half full. Old shops closing, too often leaving empty store rows.

Too many people homeless. Hopeless, helpless, hiding in alleys beside shopping cart homes.

Crime creeps along the edge like a black cat on a fence.

Too many young men willing to prey on others with violence and strife.

Change may come too late for the homeless and those caught up in crime.

Courage on the edge.

There are still many brave people caring and helping where they can.

Looking to the future. Coming up with a plan.

They are still there to lift up the weak, befriend the hopeless, and meet others' needs.

Even when terror came into a meeting of friends, the unfailing spirit of that city lived on.

And as San Bernardino climbs up from the edge, so do all those from the metropolis who look out to the edges to live.

Strange Spirits of the San Bernardino Desert

Christine Chatterton

We went out to the desert thinking there would not be much to see.

"What could live out there?" we wondered. "In the dry arroyos and rocky hills, what could there be?"

Little did we realize the desert was alive with the spirits of giants, and creatures big and small.

And spirits of long years past and even some with no shape at all.

As we walked among monoliths of rock and on high flat topped buttes, suddenly I spied

Two rock giants sleeping, but they paid us no mind. One was in a cave and one on a hillside.

We walked past the Dr. Seuss trees spreading limbs every which way.

They are called Joshua Trees, or so they say.

We came to a stream where no water would flow. Among cactus and sagebrush was a sight to see along the way.

Our notion that the land was dead was wrong, we now could tell.

The desert was in full bloom with colors of pink and blue and yellow.

We saw caterpillars by the hundreds, with green and yellow stripes, climbing, eating, wiggling all around me.

Taking care to walk around them so as not to dash their hopes to become butterflies, to finally be free.

On we walked until we reached a wall of rock blocking our way, and stood in awe at the pictures so very old.

Made long ago by warrior's hands, to show that they were there and show a story that they told.

We could almost hear a beating drum and a song upon the wind.

And we knew that ancient spirits still dwelt among those rocks, their story to begin.

The final thing we saw that day was a strange and wondrous sight..
A burning bush with a spirit flame, wavering in a dance of light.
I am not lying when I say I said a little prayer and hummed a little hymn.
We walked around the bush to see if light refracted through the limbs.
The flame burned real but cool and not consuming.
I know the desert is alive and there are more spirits there to see than we had been assuming.

First Date

Erika Ayón

We took a walk to the park, at the beginning
we discussed Frida Kahlo, politics, and soccer.
As the path winded, past the teenage skaters,
the guys playing football and several runners,
we talked about our favorite color red,
San Bernardino where you grew up,
Los Angeles where I am from.
As we sat down under a tree, we reminisced
about your time at The Catholic Worker;
how you woke up at 5 a.m. to volunteer
at the soup kitchen. How nuns cooked chilies
in the community kitchen, and the smoke
and scent cast a fog over the entire house.
The trips to Home Depot with Feliciano,
one of the residents. Feliciano who painted
propping his right hand with the left when
his shoulder was dislocated. One summer,
this same man took the chicken that someone
had built a splint for her wing to keep her alive,
and was found in the porch, surrounded
by a blanket of brown feathers. He had a pot
in front of him, held the corpse over
it like a prize, in the distance,
the sky burned orange.

I Married a San Bernardinian
Erika Ayón

Sometimes when we are asleep,
I am afraid that a mountain
will rise from within you.

Your eyelids still carry the dust
that was brought with the evening winds.
Your eyes turn grey like the smoky skies
that appeared above the school yard
when you were a child. Whole cities
surrounding San Bernardino
swept their smog into it. The smog
so unbearable they canceled P.E. class.

In your dreams, you return to your
grandfather's house on Tanner Circle.
You are six years old. You play at the back
where the orange groves used to be.
You become lost in between branches
of barren trees. Your cousin Mikey
is with you, climbing the dirt mounds
formed from skeletons of orange orchards.

In your memories, you walk down
9th street to Our Lady of Guadalupe

Shrine Church. Where you were
an altar boy. Where your grandfather
is still a deacon. Where after mass
your family would go with their own
olla and get offerings of *menudo*
from Zacatecas Café.

When we go back to visit,
off the freeway, every time you see
Mt. Vernon Ave. You find yourself,
on the passenger side of a car,
your friend Emilio at the wheel,
he drives down the hill at 75 miles
per hour on a dare, crashes
at the bottom. A fire engulfs the car.
Sometimes, in your mind
you don't make it
out of that fire.

The Moment

When he (my husband) finds out about the terrorist attack at the San Bernardino Inland Regional Center, December 2, 2015.

Erika Ayón

The moment when he heard about it,
he called everyone who still lived there,
his mom, step dad, grandparents.
Even though he knew it was highly unlikely.

There was still in his mind a chance.
They could have been passing by.
Something could have brought them there.
San Bernardino never felt so small.

The way he talked about it, I understood,
Why them? A city that had lost so much.
The economy never really bounced back.
The jobs that left didn't come back.

It's not like other cities he kept saying.
The pain was already there. The city
had been mourning, still clearing
the rubble from many earthquakes.

He refused to go and see where it happened

when we went back home to visit his family
the first Christmas after it occurred. It had
since created a volcanic sized void inside him.

He was exhausted from having to lose
another person there. Having to make space
in his mind for more of its ghosts. Having
to turn another place there into a graveyard.
He was sad that for most, this will be
the only thing they know of San Bernardino.
They won't know the way mountains
embrace the city, swallow the sky.

How indigenous tribes called it "The valley
of the cupped hand of God." How streets are carved
from stones instead of dirt. How the wind still carries
the scent of orange and olive groves from long ago.

Apartment 122
Alix Carmona

Red-eyed and softly scuffling,
Closing the door and any morning light trailing behind me.
Body turning heavier with every step
Into the somber living room.
"Living" room.

The infuriating chirping of birds,
It's time for bed.
I need to be up in a couple of hours,
With red-eyes, to stare at a white board on cream walls.
We work, we learn,
For enough money to keep a place to sleep,
A place to call "home."

My life consists of pen, paper,
And a red truck.
Traffic jams, mental-lapses.
Both create a dull, persistent,
Needle-pricking pain in my temples.

How's school? Did you get to eat?
What time do you go in to work today?
Red-eyes and quiet steps out the door,
When the moon is making its way up in the sky.

The touch of cold metal, a key,
The hum of an engine.
Another day of work and
Another day of school.

I have never been more thankful
For black-out curtains
And Red-Bull by the case.

Springtime Joshua Tree
Julie Scrivner

Casa
Nicole McDonald

There is a new vernacular here.
In between criminal neglect and child endangerment
A hope that rises from Mount Vernon.
A door for children permanently displaced in spirit
Within a system that seems insurmountable like the odds and statistics
we read
 about foster youth and graduation.
 A community that fights for the future of their very foundation.
 Holding cells butt up against courtrooms with armed officers
 Judges and social workers, attorneys in suits
 Deciding the fate of families and wards of the court
 I will hold your hand.
 You will have a voice, and a place in this room that is not a corner.
 There are many choices that don't belong to you.
 We speak about resiliency and it is the only sense that I can make out of
all of this pain.
 Breathing out hope and praying that it finds you in the dry desert air
 Or the group home that you find yourself in-
 Apart from your brother.
 I hope that you can still imagine life that isn't broken and split by addic-
tion and violence.
 That you will one day look up, and see the beauty instead of the uncer-
tainty of an unknown roof.

Lulus
Nicole McDonald

There is a dive bar in Rialto.
My confessional booth from days past-
Somewhere to sing and smoke and forget the pain of
Abandonment within a vagabond encampment.

Jerry was a biker with colon cancer.
He would sing Elvis Presley when things got to be
Too much.

And the Colonel would laugh and smelled of popcorn and Vietnam.
Glory days that faded into the bottoms of cloudy pint glasses

The women nameless, only faintly recognizable by the varying color-
ations of their
exposed
Bra straps.

Cigarette butts laid to rest in coffee cans-
This is home.
The place I longed for even as far away as London when the archaeolo-
gist would dig into me and pillage the sacred,
I imagined you were a church.
There to save me.

Coffee in Rialto

Part 1

Linda Ravenswood

especially when you're so angry it doesn't matter.

especially when you're so angry
you eat beetroots to the nub alone, standing.
especially when you're so angry everyone is yawning.
especially when you're so angry, and Gramma says
'it's a beautiful day !'
especially when you're so angry you break your feet off at the ankles
and smash about on blood stumps because
you are terror.
especially when you're so angry
at night, you flail your blood stumps
up and down, across,
and up and down, across,
and it flicks and boils and stings and burns,
and you flail the covers,
up and down flicking,
stinging, acid, burning,
but you go hard,
blood filling white sheets
by 'capillary action', thank you Sister Frances Mary

On public art and the longevity of an idea

dusk @ the San Bernardino Museum

Linda Ravenswood

If the explanation it requires
is short
or not necessary at all,
an idea can last.
So too, if its explanation
is long,
needing students
and postulators to translate
and decipher,
an idea can last -
it can endure.
But hear now -
It's the middler that's the concern;
the one without champion
the one with the gaping
hole, and folding hands,
a scrap of music from a reel to reel,
a stone chipped fragment
from a forgotten language,
someone's cherished place -
Once of the midnight drive
Once of the smiling girl by the junction

Once of the moment
real and crumbling -
he who may not find a friend
in the loping crowd
who inherits ideas from the dead.
Who will spark to the great middler,
the great *I did*
who pronounced so beautifully
his causes
into the mirror?

Twin Cities

Carlos E. Cortés

I grew up in Kansas City, Missouri,
Across the river from our twin city,
Kansas City, Kansas,
So when I looked at a map in some magazine
And saw Kansas City
I never gave a thought to
Which one was being cited
And which one was being excluded.

But when I accepted a faculty position
At the University of California, Riverside,
I quickly learned that, depending upon which map,
Riverside might be there east of Los Angeles
But sometimes it was nowhere to be found
Giving way to San Bernardino
Or maybe they, too, were considered twin cities,
And, like my two Kansas Cities,
Their individual existence was merely an illustrator's whim.

Fifty years and many maps later
Sometimes with Riverside
Sometimes with San Bernardino
Often with neither
Seldom with both

I occasionally wonder

Who makes these decisions?

Who decides whether our cities exist or become invisible?

Skaters Prevail

Tristan Acker

now you know why young Latinas of my city
walk their kids past the fountains of city hall
on the deck of the only noticeable municipal building
once you're on E Street bridge between City Hall and Carousel
all you see behind you is the statue of Martin Luther King Jr.
in front of you the murky glass mall entrance
the skaters will outlast
the enforcement of your loitering laws
the skaters will outlast
the ten businesses left in the seemingly empty mall
the skaters will outlast
the sign that reads "RADISSON CLOSED FOR RENOVATIONS" they
put up in the 90s
the skaters will outlast
M & D holdings
The roof's leak resistance and structural integrity
The Skaters Will Outlast That Too
your economic system
your Central City Shopping Center
your venture capital
the money to pay enough security to chase kids away
The Skaters Will Outlast Them All

and when you're smoking a cigarette next to the years' unused bike racks
look out at a damned-near empty parking lot
tune into the sweet-grey air silence California's January brings
All you hear is the sound of kickflips

San Bernardino Haiku
Sylvia J. Clarke

Green to brown on hills
As temperatures rise higher
I long for more rain

Fall in the Chaparral
liz gonzález

Santa Anas howl
down Cajon Pass

I sleep on the edge
my side of the bed
not to disturb, but you
snore on the couch

Gusts plow calico-
hued hillsides

Filigree bones
of a scrub jay's wing
snuggle in the shadow box
you made to save the memory

Yucca swords
slash the moonlight

A battery-operated clock
glows on the mantle
(Electricity is unreliable
during winds and quakes)

Bitter breeze whistles

through window cracks

Your Granny Smiths rot
in the glued-back-together
anniversary bowl
You don't notice the smell

Brittlebrush bows
Christmas berry slants, rattles

I scrub pomegranate specks
off the carpet
before you spot them

A coyote crouches
behind beavertail cactus
ready to pounce on a jackrabbit

We waste hours bickering,
like tumbleweeds bouncing
aimlessly in the cactus garden

Dry leaves crumble so easily
veins can't sustain them

Our tromps back and forth
shake the wood floor
startle snakes
slithering beneath the foundation

Manzanita bushes thrash
like they want to uproot and bolt

We snap our love like weak branches
cracking off eucalyptus trees
You brush shards of us
into a dust pan

Add a spark to the drying landscape
uncontrollable wildfire will result

Flames cleanse the soil
of allelopathic compounds
clear space
for new growth

Buds curl, dry on branches
Cinder does not disintegrate

We toast Thanksgiving
from opposite ends
of our new glass table

Fall quickens

Life's Flow
Michael Orlich

Thin grey clouds hang over the wide river,
its muddy rushing roar quieted to dry dust.
No sickly sweet scent of cinnamon escapes
the California Churro Corp. on this quiet Christmas day.
Fifty feet below and worlds apart
four coyotes, all identical, dance a game of dare,
neither friendly nor fierce,
with a motley foursome of flop-eared friends—
strangely different cousins.
A spike-headed speeder flies along the riverbed,
his feet never leaving the ground.
A silent, stoic raptor sits motionless, suspended
seemingly, in the thin air of its invisible perch.
The old rusty trestle crosses overhead,
its empty tracks freighted with images of another time,
when the bustle of industry could be heard inside
the hollow hulking mass of the Griffin Wheel Company.
And the dry river rushes ever on,
as families walk and talk together,
their laughter making eddies in life's flow,
now plunging over the edge,
diving downward, punishing every atom
in its wrenching, churning spray,

then pulling itself together somehow,
pressing on along its way,
like the patient plodding runner on its bank.
Gaze steady, looking out ahead,
head level, shoulders squared,
thick arms driving an energetic beat,
hands leading his labrador companions—
black as night and radiating the joy of life—
torso upright, stable,
and strong, short legs pumping,
beating out a steady rhythm,
propelling him forward, over dusty hills
as mile follows mile.
Strong legs swing out in short arcs,
as sleek black carbon-fiber blades—
where knees used to be—
cooly, silently, rhythmically slice the air,
unfeeling, but carrying the force of life
from a warm, fleshy, pounding heart
filled with the spirit of hope.

San Bernardino Streets
Michael Orlich

Baseline

I come from the west.
You have to start somewhere.
I can see straight
down this road
for miles, but not today.
The arroyo is big, empty.
A woman picks.
Walls of comfort have gaps.
Across the tracks, the Meridian.
Arroyo Valley hawks circle
the stadium.
Tacos Mexican (what other kind?),
Rico Taco, Taco Grinch, Taco Central, Tacos L, Taco Bender.
Across the great river
of north and southbound lanes,
the smog corner, the fun corner.
Quick pawn. Fame liquor.
Dollar king, dollar tree, dollar general,
all Smart and Final.
Crossing Waterman. I don't know, Jack-
Is there a way out-of-the-Box?

The road is rising.
Milk dairy. Crazy Frank's.
Auto spa, center, zone.
Universal Tires and Unified Baptists—
let them introduce you to the way.
Gina's thrift, Charlie's cars, Dale's TV, Sam's something.
Pain's corner. Wayne's RV storage. The House of Plywood.
Pepper tree restaurant.
Sam's bargains. Gina's thrift store again.
Maybe it moved already.
Sam and Gina seem to get around. (Or was it Gino?)
Welcome to High-land.
Sterling Street—still waiting for gold.
D&D furniture. The next sign explains.
Debt and Depression.
Three towers point the way—
open spaces, climbing.
Mobile homes—still.

Eternal fire is burning.
The police stand watching.
The churches sit on Church Avenue:
First United Methodist (must have beat the Baptists).
Saint Adelaide's. A graceful spire.
A proud tower. A gilded arch
against the mountain peak—

San Bernardino looms large.
Straight ahead. Above the orange blossoms.
A marker laid down.
A city laid out.
A street laid straight. Again?
You have to start somewhere.

E Street

The SBX (its name
almost exciting
for a bus) says
"out of service"—
seeming sadly wise
despite its shiny
red paint and CNG
and dedicated lanes
and high capacity
(for emptiness) in this
broad valley of open
urban spaces.
The sign
red and square
arched and gold
says 15¢ hamburgers
and a many-zeroed number sold,

but none for sale
here and now—
for what prophet
remembers his home
when profit calls?
But burgers endure
at burger-market and -mania
the little Gus
the In-'N-Out-backed
Harley man, he too riding
shiny red, without
the empty seats.
Other tarnished temples
remain and retain
or try to recall
an uncertain sanctity
of short school days
sleek, long cars
fresh, sweet citrus
and sixty-six—
remembered now by
the family service center
the Asian seafood market
NAPA's omnipresent parts
trucks and taquerias
the Indian-band ballpark

Christ, the scientist
and other vacancies,
a shrined (or coffined) carousel.
Above it all
in sparkling steel and glass
a block or two off Easy Street—
the Center of Justice.

Waterman

I travel south, the way of waters
fleeing down from the mountains,
the old Arrowhead pointing the way,
where water brought healing and hype,
where drought is bottled
and shipped for sale;
to the center of town,
the hallowed and the hollow,
with its Wienerschnitzels and wigs,
that center of dismantling
where it's legal to pick-a-part,
with bail bonds and bótanicas
for those who suffer.
The left promises to deliver
as trucks back up to
endless bays without water,

which is pumped from the ground
toward the sea it will not reach,
ions exchanged for its TCE.
Roofing tiles sit stacked, silent.
Golf greens fly flags and flowers
in mourning.
Drab green fencing
seeks to hide the horror
so fresh, foreign, familiar.
The road goes on
watered by tears,
and ends in a Little Hill
in the place of remembering.

Ms. Rivers
Michelle Bracken

You looked like you ate cherries for breakfast and as if your dad called you Buffy. I was sure you had the whitest dad, the whitest mom, and the whitest life.

But it drove me crazy sometimes how not white you were.

The time I saw you shuffle on the blacktop, the time you did the Dougie, and the Cat Daddy. That's when I knew. You were white, yeah, but the coolest white lady I ever saw. You could dance. So I went up to the principal and told her how I felt about you, and that next year, you were the only teacher I wanted. That if I couldn't have you, I would just not come to school. She looked at me, and told me to take my hat off, and to pull up my pants, and that what I really needed was a belt, not you.

You had a lot of us that year. The kids no one really wanted. The kids that some teachers would just look at and sigh. *Not those kids. No way, not in my line, my life.*

But you weren't like that. You sometimes rolled your eyes, and moved your neck like Asiana moved hers when Robert got in her face, but then you would laugh, and we would laugh, and everything would be okay.

Sometimes we thought you were crazy. Like the time you started rapping in class. I put my head down because I was so embarrassed for you. It was good, though. We really didn't know you could do that. We knew you could move, we saw it on the playground at recess, but rap, too? It was just too much.

But you just kept going, and we kept watching, and then when you were done, we didn't know what else to do but stare. And then you smiled, and said go ahead and laugh. So we did. Sometimes I would stand in line, and wish you would just talk to me, about anything. About why I hated math, or why I choose to ignore you in class, or why I brought my skateboard to school. Anything. But you would just ask me to get in line.

The time you came to my football game, though. That was cool. I didn't think you'd actually come. But I made my mom text you, and you guys talked, and one Saturday morning, there you were. That's my teacher, I told my dad. He was my coach, and you waved, and he looked at you, and looked at me, and said, that's your teacher?

That white lady? The one who looks like she's twenty?

I know, dad, I said. I looked at the field, at the grass, and didn't look at you.

You sat with my mom. And you put a dollar in the cup every time my team made a touchdown. After that, the other boys wanted you to go to their games, too. Cesar and Von, they couldn't believe it. But you came to mine first, and that mattered more than anything.

What's that? Isis asked one day.

She was pointing to a plaque you had near the white board. It wasn't very big or anything, but it stood there for most of the year, and no one said anything about it. Not even you.

It's an award, you had said.

Isis wanted to know what for, why, when, and how you got it. She was like that. She asked a lot of questions, and could remember everything you told her. She loved you, too, only it took you a long time to see it.

So you told us it was for teaching, and we thought that was pretty cool.

But there were some days when you looked like you wanted to be anywhere but school. Like when you had to tell Manny to sit down, or put his white board away, or anything. You would just all of a sudden yell Manny! and there would be this look on your face. Like you were done.

Every time we had a sub, it was bad. So bad. Sometimes you'd come back and read the note the sub left, and you would just give it to us. I could tell you were unhappy about it, but the class was terrible. You knew it. Everyone knew.

Can't you just once behave? you asked us. I couldn't tell you either way the answer to that.

Manny! Again and again, it was mostly Manny.

And then you started to get skinny. Real skinny. So skinny that one day when you took off your sweater Isis just burst out, Oh my gosh you're getting so skinny! My teacher is so skinny. And you were. You were always healthy looking, told us to eat from the salad bar, but something was different, like you weren't eating at all.

Isis just looked at you, and the class looked at the both of you.

How come you're so skinny? Isis asked. Are you eating?

We all wanted to know the answer to that. Something was off. You were different. Like your cat died or something. Von would come up and hug you at recess and ask you how you were doing, and he told me that sometimes you had tears in your eyes, and that you were going to cry and he knew it and he didn't want you to cry.

She's like my momma, he told me once. He didn't really have one of those, just his grandma who he called momma.

I can tell how she feels all the time, he told me. I can feel it deep, like right here, he said, and he was holding his stomach.

So what's wrong with her? I asked.

She's just really sad, he said. I don't know why, sometimes grownups get like that.

So we would do things to cheer you up. Crystal would give you compliments about how pretty you were, and how beautiful you looked when you danced, and that you were the best teacher ever, and that she loved you, and you would smile, and sometimes it would seem like that was all you needed to be okay.

Eari would draw you pictures, and write you letters, and make you cards, and one time she wrote a story about school and you were in it, and so was Manny, and you let her read it aloud. She called it "Summer" even though it was about school, but you didn't say anything about that, and she looked so happy when she was done reading. We all thought she was kinda strange, because sometimes she would say weird things, like a pencil was a banana or to stop looking at her, even though no one was. But on that day, everyone clapped and said good job, because you made us feel like it really was.

A month later and you were gone.

No one knew why, but Von said it was probably because you weren't eating anymore, he could tell, and that your eyes, they were different, like dark water. We had a lot of subs. Manny would run around the room with his shirt wrapped around his face like some of the gangbangers from the block, and the sub would tell him to sit down, and Manny would just keep going. He threw his chair across the room one time, and the principal had to come down and ask us if that's how you wanted us to behave. We said no, of course, and then she told us you were sick, real sick, and that even though you weren't there, you still wanted us to do our best.

The class nodded, and looked as if they would try, but it would end as soon as she'd leave. Manny would get up again, and talk to himself, and take his shoes off, and then crawl around the carpet.

The kids would laugh, and I laughed too. It was crazy.

When's she coming back? My mom asked and I told her I didn't know. She didn't like it all that much, you being gone, and she even tried calling you, but you never answered. My mom wanted me to switch classes, and work with some other teacher, but I told her you'd be back because like you said, you don't leave.

You were back after Valentine's Day. You looked the same. Real thin and real sad. You didn't dance anymore, and you stopped playing music in class. Mostly you just yelled at Manny, and kept to yourself. Eari and Crystal would knock on the door during lunch, but you didn't come out anymore.

The state test was coming up, so we did a lot of review. We set goals, and most of the class said they wanted to be proficient, but we really had no idea what that even meant.

Will we pass? We asked. We just didn't know.

Of course you will, you had said. But sometimes it'd look like you didn't know for sure.

On the day of the test, you brought us doughnuts, and told the class that those who were working hard, and trying their best, would have a treat when the time was over.

I looked around the room, and a lot of the kids were busy. I couldn't tell how you thought we did. I thought maybe I could read you, and then feel a little better about the rest, but your face was still, firm, and didn't let on either way.

Afterwards, you gave everyone a doughnut and we pigged out while watching Jackie Chan beat up some dudes in a ninja movie. After lunch you told us you couldn't do that any more because at recess Cesar kicked some second grader in the nuts. Like Jackie Chan. You didn't say nuts, but we knew what you meant.

The end of the year came fast. There were a lot of activities, and celebrations, and the class was trying to come up with something for the talent show to show you just how much we'd miss you. Von said we should sing, and bring you up on stage. She'll just love that, he had said, and the other boys seemed to agree.

We'd practice at lunch, and Crystal would pretend to be you, and she'd sit in the center, holding her arms together, and just smile like you used to. We'd sing, and sometimes laugh, and Von told us to be serious, because this was a big deal.

It's the last time on the last day we're gonna see Ms. Rivers, he had said. Don't you want it to be special? He even tried to get Manny in on it, but Manny couldn't sing, and couldn't keep his hands still. So, we had to cut him and instead Von offered him a bag of Hot Cheetos if he would just leave you alone and sit still for a day.

Don't even do anything, he had said, just let her teach.

The day before the talent show, I had forgotten my homework. So I rode my bike down the street, and saw you outside the classroom. You hadn't left for home, and I waved.

You started walking toward the back gate, and I rode my bike over to meet you.

The gate was locked.

Hi, Cord, you had said.

Hey Ms. Rivers. I forgot some math pages.

That's ok. Don't worry about it. You can do it in class tomorrow.

I got off my bike, and said that my mom wanted me to do it that night. She was strict like that.

You looked at your watch, and looked back at the room, and said okay, you had a few minutes. I watched you as you walked back to the class-room, unlocked the door, and went inside.

I could see you through the window.

You ran your hands through your hair, and just stood there for a bit, like you were trying to remember what to do. Then you grabbed your purse, went to my desk, picked up the sheets I had left, and came back to the gate.

Thanks, Ms. Rivers, I had said.

You rolled up the papers, and handed them to me through a hole in the metal fence.

No problem, see you tomorrow.

Yeah, tomorrow.

Only tomorrow came and you didn't. You were gone again, and on the last day. The class started booing when the sub showed up, and no one wanted to do the song. Crystal said we still had to do it, and that she'd take your place.

So, we went up on stage, and sang to Crystal, and tried to pretend it was you. Von gave her a sunflower because you told him that was your favorite, and his grandma took a picture. The day was over in a flash, and we took our things and said our goodbyes. Over the summer there were lots of rumors about you. Some of the kids in the neighborhood said you got shot up like JoJo at Del Taco. I didn't really want to hear all of that, and just told myself that you went off to some other school.

I went to a different school the following year, and so did Von. We ended up taking the bus to another academy, and on the ride home sometimes we'd talk about you.

Why do you think we miss her so much? he asked once.

It's like your dog, I told him. You know, the one you had stolen? When things are torn like that, it's hard to let them go.

Who says you have to? Von asked.

So, don't, I told him. Don't.

When Later Sounds Like Love
Casandra López

She wasn't there when it happened. Didn't even feel a premonition. No gasp of sudden breath waking her from a deep sleep or an uneasy feeling lodged within her stomach. Later she would hear all of the stories, multiple versions of possibility. And for each version she heard, from the police, the doctors, his friends, she couldn't help to think that she could have stopped those bullets. Stopped them from invading, ripping into her son, her only child. Oh, maybe he wasn't a child anymore, long past the age where he could fit in her lap and be rocked. He had grown large and strong, calloused hands making a life for himself. He was not quite as large as his own father had once been before sickness had taken him years before. But now they both lay together side by side becoming grass and stone, without her.

It was months ago. Now the days have become clearer, more distinct instead of a wide field of pain. Her son shared a place with his girlfriend, but she liked to remind him not forget that this was home too, she was home. She last saw him on a summer night when he came for dinner still in his orange work shirt, a faint glimmer of sweat on his forehead. He washed his hands with a thick milky soap she kept in the kitchen, just for him. Hands that would later grasp her shoulders in a tight hug from behind. She reminded him to take food home.

"It will go bad here," she said reaching for the plastic containers.

"Okay, Little Mama," he said, moving toward her, so that he was looking down at the crown of her head from above, smiling at her as if he had birthed her and not the other way around.

She looked up at him and said, "Your hair is getting longer." Meaning it that time only as an observation, like a remark about the heat of the day. She regretted her words as he backed away from her, crooking his neck to his shoulder, one hand running through the hair above his ear. What did he hear in her words, she wondered.

He took the containers from her hand and said, "Thanks. See ya later."

"Later," she said back.

It is those last words that won't leave her, she breaks them apart, rolls the sounds on her tongue, touches the tip to top of her mouth, attempting to make, "Later" sound like "Love."

It seems impossible that he had survived his wild teenage years when the street life held an allure, but not that night. How many times had she told him, half jokingly, half seriously that he couldn't outrun a bullet, not at his size – all broad shouldered with his slow stroll. And really who could, except in movies. She had watched him mellow into life. "Hardworking" was how his supervisor described him as he clutched her hand at the memorial service. The whole time all she could think about was that it didn't seem right that he would be the one chosen from a group of breathing bodies by a blind bullet.

That night is now shocked into her memory forever. She imagines the details all the time. The pieces that she has to fit together. He was at a car show in a park with his girlfriend and some friends. The summer was coming to the end, bringing a light breeze, masking the tension. Maybe he didn't sense it until seconds before, his street senses dulled by music and the foaming amber liquid in his red plastic cup. There must have been a gasp from the crowd, thick with bodies, the silencing of the music in his head as he focused in on surprised faces; the flashing and blurring of clothing. She tells herself, he didn't feel pain. She tells herself that she is not the only one who thinks that later can sound like love.

Jeremiah Gilbert

Jeremiah Gilbert

SAN BERNARDINO, SINGING

Jeremiah Gilbert

SAN BERNARDINO, SINGING

Jeremiah Gilbert

Jeremiah Gilbert

SAN BERNARDINO, SINGING

Jeremiah Gilbert

SAN BERNARDINO, SINGING

149

Jeremiah Gilbert

SAN BERNARDINO, SINGING

Jeremiah Gilbert

SAN BERNARDINO, SINGING

Jeremiah Gilbert

SAN BERNARDINO, SINGING

Jeremiah Gilbert

SAN BERNARDINO, SINGING

Jeremiah Gilbert

SAN BERNARDINO, SINGING

An Inland Empire Girl

Juanita E. Mantz

I am an Inland Empire Girl
Born in Great Falls, Montana
Moved here when I was three

I am a OG 909er
who loves her hometown
I grew up in Onterrible

Now I live in San Bernardino
I came home after years of running
To LA, Houston, San Francisco

I came home to find myself
I came home to love myself
I came home to remember

I am an Inland Empire Girl
And you can't talk bad about my hometown
Unless you're from here
But even us old timers need to stop
Because we are beautiful people
Of all colors and creeds

San Bernardino is a beautiful place
Where oranges and vineyards once reigned

Juanita E. Mantz

Where the first McDonalds was built

A decade ago I came home
To heal from my father's passing
Now I grieve for my city

Genevieve Street
Adam Martinez

On early evenings, a woman and her son would walk several blocks to buy groceries. Food stamps kept him fed a few times. Passing streetlights with a tangerine glow, the fire station to the right, an empty elementary on the left. Trees with low-hanging leaves and shoes tangled in power lines, housing project apartment complexes. A bar where the boy would eventually spend nights with friends fending off feelings of inferiority with a few beers and a laugh. The boy and mom would walk home, arms weighted with grocery bags. Outside, in a sad city, walking with his mother, the boy felt safe.

Easter Sunday
Adam Martinez

We own land. By land, I mean several plots for passing. Solving mysteries
near mausoleums in spring. There is sun. There are occasional clouds and
a cool breeze. All is quiet and calm and pinwheels spin while pink, yellow,
and white petals on tulips twitch and jiggle over neatly trimmed grass surrounding memorial plaques.

Every Easter I,
with my mother and father,
bring flowers to my mother's mother and father—
Grandma Katy and Grandpa "Mago".
My great-grandfather, her grandfather, his father-in-law
was a sheriff deputy of San Bernardino County
in the '40s or '50s.
Frank F. Delgado is news to me.
He kept my city safe
for my grandfather
to raise my mother
to raise me.

My mother told me Mago changed after Grandma Katy died. Every Easter, Grandma Katy told Mago not to cut the grass so the kids could hunt
for eggs but he hated the mess. When Grandma Katy died, he stopped
cutting it and his grandkids would visit to search for pastel-colored eggs
filled with confetti, and break them on each other's head.

Santa Fe Whistle

Adam Martinez

I've roved around but here you remain
in the same bed you've slept in
all these years I'm reminded upon return

death is near
home is queer after awhile
it no longer exists

you just float along
like stagnant water in urban lakes
or putrid ponds

where people pour pollution
and graffiti lines the public restroom walls
clear signs of a poor economy

A few miles from where
Mago sleeps
sits Seccombe Lake

Once a pristine park near
a presently dilapidated
Downtown San Bernardino

My parents took me to feed the ducks

old hard bread now a haven
for vagrants vandalism and violent crimes

druggies and hoes earn cash
in an urn with ash, divers comb the muck
for evidence of a holy war

Mago made a living
working many years
at Santa Fe Depot

I miss hearing that whistle blow.

Not from Moscow
Dane Rigsby

March 3, 1975 was the date. My family and I had moved out of the L.A. area and the crime that came with living there. I was 7 years old, my sister Brandi was 6. My parents bought a 10 acre ranch in an unincorporated area just outside the westside community of Muscoy. Located on Gray Street just off of Cajon Boulevard it was definitely rural, with no streetlights or paved roads. The first day was great as my sister and I were driven to and from school. The day ended with root beer floats at the A&W on Highland Avenue. Unfortunately that was the last ride my parents ever gave me to school.

Covering our shoes and pants legs with trash bags to cross the flood control channel became standard operating procedure. One year in the late 70's it rained for 2 weeks straight forcing us to find a different means to cross. The trains used a bridge at the end of the channel so we decided to give it a shot. As we crossed the bridge I noticed something so surreal as to never be forgotten. A horse was being swept away by the raging torrent in the riverbed.

It's hard to imagine anything being able to survive such a swift and powerful current. Many years later a runaway train would cross that same bridge before derailing into several homes on Darby Street. An underground pipeline carrying jet fuel would also be damaged by the train derailment. The pipeline would later explode as transport of the product was restarted. Tragically several people lost their lives in these two incidents.

The teachers at Vermont Elementary School in Muscoy always made me feel as though my education was important. In the 6th grade I wrote an essay on what education meant to me. In the paper I said that education was the future. One could do great things and go as far as their education. I still strongly believe a person's potential can be reached through education and training.

Well someone seemed to appreciate my essay and decided to give me a trophy for scholastic achievement. A hard cover notebook was thrown in to boot. The only bad part was that I had to receive the award in front of the entire school at assembly. I prepared a brief speech and even had my 3X5 cards ready. I was taking this whole thing quite seriously. Thankfully, everything went off without a hitch. I thanked my parents and teachers for helping me earn the award. The best part came later as my dad complimented me on my speech. That made it all worthwhile.

As I grew older I would sometimes hear people derisively refer to the community I grew up in as Moscow. Some folks from the L.A. or Orange County areas would mention I.E. people. I never did understand that type of talk. I never believed that where someone came from should define them. One's intellect, character, and his or her abilities are much more important than where they reside.

Although I moved away in 2004 I always look forward to the times when I return to San Bernardino. Rosa Maria's still makes the best pork burrito I've ever eaten and Mongolian BBQ on Del Rosa and Highland is the best meal in the entire Southland. There are still so many great things to do and see. From attending a musical or play at the Perris Hill Bowl or California theatre to attending a minor league baseball game downtown. Seeing a great concert in Devore is never a bad choice.

Never forgetting that there are still men and women who care about this town. Our hometown San Bernardino.

Sweethearts

Westside 1926

liz gonzález

Oh, I was ready for him that afternoon.

My parents stepped outside the store to take my little brothers and sisters to the fiesta at the park up the street, and I followed them to the front walk with the broom. I swept and watched them until they were two blocks away. Then I glanced out of the corner of my eye toward John's house across the street and saw him peeking through his front window. He knew it would be safe to come and talk to me.

I walked back inside the store, slow, like nothing was happening. Once inside, I ran across the store into the stockroom. I pulled out the clothes I had hidden behind some boxes and changed out of my apron and work dress. As fast as I could, I stepped into my prettiest dress: maroon with a pleated skirt. Mama had made it for me for Christmas. My fingers trembled, making it hard to fasten the hooks and eyes on the side of my dress. It was chilly in the store, but I didn't have to cover up my dress with a sweater. I was hot from the excitement. Next, I slipped on my good black shoes with a heel to make me tall and slim.

Standing in front of the mirror hanging on the wall, I painted pomegranate red lipstick on my lips and rubbed some onto my cheeks. I wiped my index finger on the soot I collected in an empty matchbox and brushed the soot on my eyelashes. I was fixing one of my ringlets when I heard the bell on the front door tinkle.

My heart pounded so hard I thought it would break my ribs open. After months of sending letters to each other through my best friend Vicky, we were going to talk for the first time. One part of me felt confident. Out of all the pretty girls in the neighborhood, he wanted to court me. The other part of me worried he might think I was too dumb and unsophisticated for him. He went to high school and had experienced life in other states and Mexico. My parents made me quit school after sixth grade, and except for trips to Westminster and Long Beach to see my cousins, all I knew was San Bernardino.

Pretending not to see him, I walked to the front counter. He was picking oranges out of a crate beneath the front window, squeezing them, as though he was trying to find a good one. He wore a dark blue suit with a royal blue necktie. A royal blue hankie stuck out of his pocket. His thick, wavy hair was slicked back with pomade, and he was clean-shaven. None of the boys in my neighborhood dressed so good.

"There you are." He spoke good English, like Vicky said, and smiled so big the top of his gums showed.

I felt dizzy. I grabbed a dust rag from under the counter and turned my back to him and dusted the vegetable cans on the shelves. "Can I help you?"

"Will you face me, please?" His voice was gentle.

I turned around too fast. He was leaning over the counter, and I almost bumped his nose with mine. He smelled clean, like shaving cream and soap. We both gasped and stepped back.

"What can I do for you?" I did my best to sound calm.

"I thought Vicky told you I wanted to talk to you."

He wasn't good looking with those tiny crow eyes and that crooked beak nose, but he made me feel like fainting. I couldn't talk and rubbed an invisible smudge on the counter.

Sra. Molina, the old widow who lived next door, opened the store door, startling us.

"Buenos tardes," she said and joined us at the counter.

"Buenas tardes, Sra." John stepped aside, waving his hand from her to the counter. "Passe usted."

His heels knocked on the wood floor as he walked back to the crate of oranges. It seemed that every step announced that we had been alone together. Sra. Molina asked for a pound of beans. My hands shook as I poured them into a paper bag. Everyone in the neighborhood had gone to the fiesta. I didn't realize she might stay home. If she told my father about John, he would beat me with his belt. She paid for the beans and left like everything was fine, but I worried.

John hurried back and spoke in English again. "That was a close call."

I rubbed the invisible smudge.

His eyes opened wide and his smile curled down, like he was frightened. "Did I do something wrong?"

"Oh, no." I shook my head. "You can't stay. Someone might tell my father."

"Give me five minutes, please? I've waited a long time for us to meet."

His smile and sweet voice made me feel comfortable. If Sra. Molina was going to tell my dad, I might as well make the beating worth it. I stopped cleaning the counter and looked up at him. "Okay," I said.

"I want to know all about you. Where did you grow up?"

"Here, on this corner, but I didn't always live here." I told him about the beautiful year we lived in Meadowbrook when I was ten, the boy who drowned when the creek flooded, and Mama insisting we move back to the Westside. I also told him about the day Papá broke my heart when he said I couldn't go to junior high because Mama needed me to help her run the store. I never talked about these things with anyone, not even Vicky, but with John, it felt good.

He gently rested his hand on mine. "I'm sorry you had a hard time," he said.

A warm feeling spread over me.

"And you?" I asked. The palm of his hand was wet. I hoped he was nervous too.

He smiled his gummy smile, stood straight, and talked like he was giving a speech. "I went to the High School of Commerce in Omaha, Nebraska, and played clarinet in the band and was on the debate team. Omaha, that's where I grew up."

I was too embarrassed to ask what a clarinet and debate were, but I liked that he was trying to impress me.

Some kids ran by the store, laughing and talking. They were probably coming back from the fiesta. I looked out the front window. Dark gray clouds were taking over the sky. My family would be home soon, and I needed time to change and wash off my makeup.

"You have to go."

I had some candy, those tiny hearts, in a red glass bowl on the counter for sale. He picked up one, looked at it, and smiled at me, hugging me with his eyes: "I love you."

Then he handed the heart to me.

I read it, and that's what it said: "I love you." I couldn't believe it; the first one he chose.

"I love *you*," I said and ate it.

Verdolagas

Juan Delgado
with images by Thomas McGovern

1.

Prelude: Cosmopolitan Weed

Your seeds were among other fossils in the soil of villages.
You grew among the native corn fields across the Americas.
There is no fencing-in your wonder, your Pre-Columbian pollen.
Like so many, you're a transplant—your tear-shaped leaves,
your purple-red stems, and your blooming yellow flowers.

In the empty fields of our barrio, we could spot you widening
the cracks of our sidewalks into gardens. You thrive beyond
our backyard fences—we reject names like "illegal" or "alien."
Persistence is one of your beauties; we know the mind-link
fences and their woven-in policies will not block you from us.

In the Americas, los abandonados jump over a fence,
a barking dog, a border that moved on them, a recliner
floating into the glow of a TV screen wide as a lion's mouth,
a blouse half-buried in the mud of an unfinished pilgrimage,
a politician smoking weed for the joint pain of his hinged knees,
and the blooming and tugging of a road's broken yellow lines.

2.

Song: Read in Four Ways

                                      Hey,

that girl walking past

another barrio   lot de   verdolagas

                abandonado

sings that niños

blancos y marrones,   perdidos y encontrados

know that   sprawling

hierba.

                That dog   is

                guarding la misma gate,

                barking as if we're not   already

                    beyond the fencing with you.

Let's savor   around us.

Little Hogweed

Juan Delgado with images by Thomas McGovern

Verdolaga

Purslane

Baldroega

San Berdoo, Somewhat Randomly
Katherine Cech Latonio

I've often wondered how much the geography of a place maps the geography of our hearts. A huge part of my own geography surely comes from this place in which I have spent so much of my life. And so here, a somewhat random visit:

A Wisconsin transplant, a product of 70s divorced parents whose clinically depressed mother read Betty Friedan and professor father romanced his secretary over two martini lunches, arriving in Rialto to a flat-roofed house on a slab on the corner of Eucalyptus and Baseline with manicured dichondra grass lawn and towering date palms, I didn't have a clue about this place of hot, dry brown landscapes and hot, dry brown air.

Enrolled at Frisbie Jr. High where I was dressed Midwestern wrong, the soc's rejected me and the Black and Chicana girls delighted in taunting me, an easy target with my freckled face and skinny five shades too white legs, schlepping an uncool violin to school and eating brown paper bag lunches, somehow I made friends and found my place.

Needing more space than our grandmother's house could provide, we ended up with a San Bernardino address when our mother bought a house perched on "the bench" above the Lytle Creek wash between Rialto and Muscoy from her brother who was trading up to the foothills above Arrowhead Country Club.

I grew to love that low-slung ranch-style house with its breezeway between the house and the garage and mini orange grove for a backyard, the dusty hillocks and train tracks in the wash which I could see from our front lawn, and the Santa Ana's whipping through the acacia and eucalyptus trees seemingly able to carry with them my teenage angst and anxiety if only for a short while.

At the urging of my more talented cousin—but with no previous practice or instruction—I tried out for Junior University on a concrete stage canopied by towering oaks at Perris Hill Park, singing "A Time for Us" from Franco Zefferreli's Romeo and Juliet with wobbly knees and shaky voice and not surprisingly was not chosen (though she later was). It was one of many instances of me feeling like a "poor relation" who didn't quite fit into my new landscape, but I liked the park.

After an unfortunate leap in a long jump event, I spent my 15th birthday laid-up in a ward with 4 and 7 year olds at St. Bernadine's Hospital on Highland and Waterman where I was supposed to pee into a bed pan without the privacy a curtain might have afforded me, doubly humiliated because they must have taken me for a much younger child.

On some Saturdays, my sister and I caught the city bus on Foothill (not far from the Wigwam motel) to Central City Mall—"the Mall that has it all, you're going to find, la, la, what you're looking for-or–or . . ." —where my sister and I shopped at Harris Co. pretending we were wealthy aristocrats as we ascended its regal curving staircase—if we saved our allowances long enough—or Penneys or Montgomery Wards if we didn't.

Unable to afford the Mary Lyn dance studio that the cooler girls studied at, my sister and I took modern jazz dance lessons at Bernice's studio, a converted bungalow with rough and uneven hardwood floors on Mt. Vernon just over the bridge south of Foothill. Afterwards, with anxiety and trepidation, we walked a gauntlet past homeless guys and drunks down 2nd Street and under the freeway to D Street where our mother worked in our uncle's appraisal office.

One year, having met some level of dance proficiency, we performed to a Three Dog Night song on a side stage at the Orange Show in our green and orange fringed costumes without the white go-go boots that Bernice insisted we needed but couldn't afford, while a few passers-by looked on.

Afterwards, walking the midway and wishing we had boyfriends to win the giant Pandas for us and therefore forced to waste our own quarters on ring tosses and ball throws, we cooled off in the exhibit halls filled with all things orange, handmade and homegrown, then hit the rides, getting mildly sick on the Scramblr and Tilt-a-Whirl, only to do it all over again.

All our home football games took place there too, Eisenhower High being too small yet to afford its own stadium, and it was there on a Halloween night that I flirted with the cute guy from history class with long curly hair and dark skin who kissed me the first time in King Arthur's Pizza on Baseline after the game and later became my boyfriend, husband and father of my son, and then even later my ex-husband.

I landed my first job at Thrifty Drug out on Del Rosa and Highland (through some connection to Uncle Duke) where two good-looking Iranians made passes at me and one locked me in the freezer and forced kisses on me, and the newly hired box boys made more than the tough grey-haired gals who had worked there for 15 years. I worked the 6-10 shift on weeknights and then fell asleep face down on my bed without taking off my clothes, though I did enjoy the 10 cent scoops of Rocky Road ice-cream and the small paychecks which bought me Ditto jeans and Electric Light Orchestra cassettes.

In the summer after I graduated from high school, working fulltime and preferring solitude to the fraught breakroom back at Thrifty's, I remembered the massive oaks of Perris Hill Park and took my lunch breaks in the shade of one particularly stately specimen, eating Filet-O-Fish sandwiches from the MacDonald's down the street and reading novels.

We spent Easters and Thanksgivings up on David Way at my uncle's swanky new place until it and everything in it burned down in the 1980 Panorama fire including our pianist grandfather's grand piano and our great-great grandfather's slightly well-known paintings, and then at the split-level condo he built over on Lomas Privadas Drive until it burned down in the 2003 Old Fire, though by then he didn't have anything left of much sentimental value.

During our college years, I traversed the west-side in the middle of some nights in my boyfriend's van keeping him company while he delivered Sun Telegram bundles, and every Wednesday we'd go to the Sun Telegram offices on D Street and pick up his paycheck and then splurge on lunch at Luv'm Burgers which my uncle owned and at which my sister and brother worked at various times during their high school and college years.

We got accessories for our Halloween costumes in yearly treks to the Fun Corner and had lunch afterwards at Sage's. My sister's psychologist was up on G Street, my first gynecologist was somewhere over there too, and the cross-town freeway was where I got my first speeding ticket.

I almost forgot that I also got married in San Bernardino (the second time). A colleague and dear friend always remarked that her backyard would be a perfect place for a wedding and, when—after years of being single—I was ready to marry again, I took her up on her offer. It was actually the perfect place for a wedding, but, sadly, her house also burned down in the Old Fire.

Our Lady of the Rosary Cathedral was my mother's church in her later years when she lived on Genevieve Street and was a member of Catholic Daughters. I dutifully attended fashion shows and bingo luncheons for years until the year she became their regent but was also found to have a brain tumor.

So San Bernardino is where my sister and I cared for our mother before she died, driving nearly daily from my job in Fontana and on the weekends from my home in Riverside, passing all the familiar and comforting landmarks that I'd known for over forty years but which now became the backdrop to my every worry—the drive wearing me down, even as my heart was being worn down with fear, and later, grief.

My husband and I have been dancing at the Brandin' Iron on E Street many Saturday nights for the last seven years, quite surprisingly, for we both never cared for country western music. It's a friendly place though with lots of regulars, and it's just down the street from the Chevron station on Orange Show Road and E Street where my brother worked to put himself through college which is down the street from the animal shelter where my mom adopted her dog Miss Merry in 1995 when her own mother died and whose demise in 2012 left her bereft and most assuredly accelerated her own decline.

The landmarks and landscapes of San Bernardino haven't remained static, and neither have I. But even though some of the landmarks I saw from the window on the city bus in 1972 may not be so different from those I passed on my drive to Genevieve Street, my own changing geography has revised how I see her geography, and I understand that there is some kind of relationship between places and people that can't be accounted for easily in words. There is something intertwining and reactive on both sides. San Berdoo gets under your skin, every place etched with a memory or connected to a memory which takes you to another memory which brought you from who you were to who you are now and who you might become.

San Bernardino
Jessie Salazar

Deep valleys nestle,
Arrowhead's living desert
Big Bear soars above.
Pop, pop; bang; PahKat.
Inland Regional Center.
North Park. Street Corner.
At dusk June bugs buzz.
One-hundred-degree weather,
Barbecue blazing.
Waterman. Kendall.
Mount Vernon. Tippecanoe.
Hospitality.
Orange Show fair rain,
a local superstition.
Laughs, rides, kettle corn.
Homicides, gangs, rape,
whispers of bankruptcy, debt,
poverty stricken.
My one-year-old niece,
all smiles, asking "what dat"
big brown eyes stare out.

4th of July: San Bernardino 2015
Casandra López

South of the freeway fireworks spit
out the whole of July.
Booms blare louder than backfires,
thundering into sky.
My friend says, no one cares if we burn
ourselves down here.
Past 30th we spark and catch fire
so easily.
We brittle as palm leaves; we dry as
brush and concrete.
Here on 10th, we prop up cannons on
poles of chain-link fences.
Here on 10th, dogs howl or cower as
fire hungry teens slow
cars with their jolting limbs crashing into
each other in the center
of the street like this is the center
of the world.
I'm always leaving, but this still remains
the center of my world,
my sun center, hottest part of ache,
my core of joy. Sometimes
it is too much and I have to shield

my vision, where I pain
easily. This is the concrete, asphalt and
chain-link Brother and I grew from.
When Brother tattooed this street
into his arm Mother thought:
now he would never leave. This was partial
truth. This street, these numbers
had dug their way into his ruddy skin
since birth.
As a boy before cell phones chirped, buzzed or
pinged he'd call to his friends
down the street with a high pitched animal whistle.
This is the way 10th sings
city, sings of lives undiagnosed of witness and
hurt. Even the dogs learn this tune.
It's been four years since Brother's murder,
and I ask myself:
when will I be post of post-traumatic?
Post guilt, post disturbance,
post fireworks sounding only like fireworks?
I try to enjoy Youngest Nephew's
face as Uncle wows him by lighting
fireworks, puncturing open the night,
marking 10th with smoke and light.
Tonight I only see faces bright
with smiles and think nothing of
flag or country.

Magnolia Ave, San Bernardino, CA

CelenaDiana Bumpus

"Then with cracked hands
That ached from labor"
She turned on the faucet
watching the water
pour from the spout,
first brown,
then tan,
then milky,
then clear.
Looked at her hands,
the roughened
white lines.
Bemused they were her hands.
She thought back
to when lotion was not a luxury,
then shook off the memory.
There was more work to do.
She scrubbed her hands clean.

Skin
CelenaDiana Bumpus

This skin of mine is a moody
mercurial creature unforgiving
and empathic, cracked like a tundra.
Compulsively I sanitize, fearing
germs and bacteria in every random
and familiar handshake, every smooth
and rounded surface. Though I rarely
remember to moisturize. Leaving my hands
resembling the barren, brown hills
of the valley I live in.

Conversely most people remark on
my face, how young I look to be forty-five.
My mother-in-law used to call me
"Baby face". Unlike my aged hands,
my face remains unmarked by the dryness
plaguing most desert-dwellers, often
masking my mercurial, ancient soul.

Lo Siento
CelenaDiana Bumpus

Stop midstride

Spinning on my favorite black Aldos
Soft solid thump nearly buckles left knee
At my feet laughing arms waving merrily
Breathless mother collects wriggling yellow stripes
Cafe de leche hand smoothes straight dark hair
Our smiling eyes meet
Lamento lo que

Poems from Muscoy

Irene Sanchez

1.

I remember the days I woke up
To taste the dusty air
Sometimes I almost choked

Sip of water from the nightstand
And I rolled over to see
Foil on the windows
That never kept the heat out

The sun stings
But I don't feel it

Fire has raised me
Here

A grown woman who isn't grown
I spent my early 20s being raised in
Muscoy

I think about how perhaps
I still haven't learned to use
What this land has taught me

Perhaps I have been afraid
Knowing that if I want to
I can rise gradually and gracefully
Like the hawks overhead

Circling the places

These places I will always fly back to
To rest
To call home

2.

My regular
Badge and Gun
San Bernardino Sheriff
Walked in one morning and asked
"What part of San Bernardino do you live in?"

Chicana barista in community college
Trying to pay for school
Living with her high school sweetheart's parents

I set his coffee on the counter
"Muscoy", I proudly said

"I would never let my daughter live THERE".

I took his money
Reserved the right to remain silent

Because I didn't have to ask
What he meant
I already knew
Mexican
Latino
Immigrant

No sidewalks
No streetlights
Drive bys

Low performance so called failing schools
But I learned there are some things that can't be
Measured in statistics and numbers

The things you won't read about in the newspapers
Are the things that are the most important
There are people who live life
In places where people don't know
Where it is
Unless you lived there
And live there
And loved there
I did
We did

3.

I hear a mother who is not my own
Cooking in the distance
I hear a mother who became my own
Yell that the frijoles are ready

Outside a cow moos
Tied up in a neighbor's front yard
We had chickens and goats in our back one

Paleteros
Elote men
Fruit trucks

Bells clanging
Calling
Bells clanging
Calling

I remember the hardest part about leaving
Was the dreadful feeling
I wouldn't come back

But every time that bells rings
No matter where
A Chicana remembers where she is from

Irene Sanchez

And every time she cooks her own pot of beans
On a hot day
She tastes
Home

The Runt Tree
Deenaz Coachbuilder

I saved you again today from being dug up and discarded,
Magnolia with stunted limbs and scraggly leaves struggling to unfold,
so dear to me. You were one of nine healthy and flourishing trees,
planted in an imposing row against the gleaming backyard fence.

All your relatives are resplendent of foliage, the burnt umber underside
of their leaves contrasting sharply against their shiny sap green fronts
pagoda like seed pods bursting with potential life
swaying and chanting a hushed song in the summer breeze.

Your leaves chatter and shiver. Your slim trunk shudders
as if a gale were buffeting your very existence.
Shorter than your companions, you paint an uneven skyline,
marring the carefully planned symmetry of the garden.
Not a tonic of Vitamin B, nor an extra dose of cool, life giving water
makes a difference, your shy diffident spirit hidden and
almost forgotten, eclipsed between the vigor of the others.

I am aware of you, inexplicably, your difference a magnet.
I sense how valiantly you try, your continued existence an anomaly.

I too had young students who attended a school[1] I worked in,
neglected at home, living in the midst of unpredictability. No kiss
ushered them to school in the morning, hidden in a pocket

---

[1] school-the writer is a retired principal of an Alternative Education School in San Bernardino, California

a *Fravashi,*[2] a good spirit to guide them through the day.
One young student's brother was shot and killed as they
rode their bicycles, close to home. One's father was in prison,
another's just...missing. One young man was being reared
by a great grandmother. They adored each other. She would attend
all parent trainings, falling gently to sleep slumped against my shoulder
as the discussion unfolded.

Some came to visit us after graduating, sensing that behind our smiles
was a silent prayer,

        as is mine for you, Magnolia.

---

[2]   Zoroastrians believe that every being has a Fravashi, a guardian angel that guides one along the right
path

The Tooth Fairy
Deenaz Coachbuilder

The tumult of the breaking school day swirls
through the halls of this alternate school campus.
Laurie, a young lady labeled "high functioning" calls out
"I'm assisting the handicapped" as she helpfully
wheels her friend's chair from the bus
into a specially designed classroom.

Broad shouldered Tony flaps his hands held in front of him
as he saunters in. He can read, but cannot smile,
ancient wisdom lines his brows.
Some I recognize by the sounds they make
not quite words, but I understand.
Sometimes they let me climb into their world.
Sometimes theirs is a lonely fortress

Here comes Joe, running into the front office
from a separate section of the building.
Recently expelled for carrying a gun
in his worn back pack, he is on loan to me
for a precious defining year. Then,
he must return to his home school.

A six year old angel. Glorious curls, eyes with the glow
of smoldering bronze, delicate features,
a naughtiness begging to be noticed.

"My tooth is falling out Miss Mary," he proudly declares.
"Let me shake it," she says, and together they tug out
this beautiful pearl white milk tooth.

Mary, the clerk, seals it in an envelope.
"Place it under your pillow so the tooth fairy
can visit you tonight."
Unfamiliar with tooth fairies he is full of wonder.

I found him sitting on the cement curb
when I drove in that morning, parking
in the usual principal's reserved spot.
"I thought I had missed the bus, so I walked to school."
He had walked a long way.
We gave him breakfast, and then, a second breakfast,
before I accompanied him to his classroom.

Mid morning Mary and I realize our mistake.
During Joe's break, we quietly exchange the envelope
hidden in anticipation, within the turmoil
of his desk, before he can transport it home.
Inside this one is a dollar.

A while later the whirlwind visits us, first Miss Mary,
then he runs into my room, to share this unusual event,

  a gift.
I hug him.

It must all come out well in the end,
it must.

That comfortless,
 Joe will learn to comfort his own.
That wordless,
 they will find a song to sing.

Thirty Nine

Vanessa Nunez

Cecilia knew her classmate was dead when the *San Bernardino Sun* released news of a young man having been shot to death in a drive-by shooting, marking it the thirty-ninth homicide of the year. No name, he was simply number thirty-nine. San Bernardino police suspect gang tensions may have had a role, just like every other murder that happens there. Thirty-nine wasn't an official member of any gang, though his brother was known to hang around a bad crowd that were suspected member of one. It was connection enough for Thirty-nine to be whispered about in school the next day, his so-called friends declaring to all that would lend an ear that they knew he was a no-good person that was asking for it.

"I heard his brother was there and left as soon as the shots started," his now ex-girlfriend said. She never shed a tear for her dead boyfriend and barely concealed her cringes every time a student gave their condolences. Thirty-nine cheated on her a total of three times before she finally broke things off with him, but that only lasted a semester before she let him back into her life. Cecilia briefly wondered if she had reacted at all to the news of her boyfriend's murder and only looked stone-faced because she'd already shed tears to the point where she could no longer produce them.

Staff had yet to receive an email from administration

about what had occurred, so the teachers refused to acknowledge Thirty-nine's empty seat, despite the constant whispering that made it clear everyone knew he wasn't just temporarily absent, he was gone for good. A bullet to the head was what killed him, but a second and third bullet plugged his right thigh and stomach. The *San Bernardino Sun* promised to update their story and release new information about the murder, but they never did, which didn't surprise Cecilia one bit. All that mattered was that some kid got killed and that he was just some punk kid in a gang. Young people died on the streets all the time; if there was any indication they were gang affiliated, then it was treated like nature was simply cleaning the dirt off the streets.

Cecilia was not friends with Thirty-nine. In fact, she hardly knew him, despite sitting next him in math for the past year, but she was confident he wasn't as bad as everyone made him out to be now that he was dead. His friends and peers knew him well enough to realize he wasn't following the same path as his older brother. It was plain to see when he'd declared to all that would hear that he planned to leave everything and everyone behind and go off to make something of himself.

His friends and older brother found that uproarious, but he appeared taller in Cecilia's eyes.

"Going to leave my shit brother and everyone else after all this," he said. "Maybe go to UCLA and study something." His best friend, Donny, grinned at that, but seeing Thirty-nine speak of such things while doing trig, Cecilia saw that he wasn't just saying these things. He truly believed them.

"Are you going to come back?" she asked.

"Nah, who knows? Maybe I'll settle down right after college, but it sure as hell isn't going to be anywhere near this damn place."

"S'not so bad," Cecilia murmured. She had no idea why she felt embarrassed saying those words, she only knew that she didn't like the look he gave her, like he was looking down at her for simply acknowledging the place as something it wasn't.

"You planning on staying here?" he inquired.

The truth was she didn't know what she planned to do after high school, and not trusting herself to say something, she shrugged, pretending to immerse herself in her trig assignment.

That was only three days before he'd been murdered. Thirty-nine was a high school Junior that had already planned for college and never got close to high school graduation.

The identity of Thirty-nine was confirmed through social media before the San Bernardino Sun had even released the article. All it took was one Tweet, a message that simply read, "Long live" and a terribly centered photograph of Thirty-nine and a friend that originally downplayed his presence in Thirty-nine's life. Twitter and Facebook soon was filled with the circulating news, the hashtags of #longlive #RIPKing #RestInPeaceK became long lists of tags used to become part of a longer conversation. All excuses to distance themselves from Thirty-nine's identity but still giving themselves a sense of authority over the topic. Instead of lashing out at his older brother for getting him involved, they lend him a shoulder to lean on, made him out to be the mourning brother, when he was now living in fear of getting himself killed. Thirty-nine was the dead punk kid while his brother was the poor older sibling that couldn't have known what his mistakes would bring.

Cecilia never spoke to his older brother, but she knew enough from the days Thirty-nine would mutter to himself during trig. His silent fuming seemed to spark his determination to graduate with top notch grades to ensure his one-way ticket out of there. She never approached him about the topic of his brother, and he never brought it up to others. There was never any loving anger when he hissed about his fucked up older brother underneath his breath, only pure hatred.

"Get himself killed," he seethed. And it is remembering that moment that Cecilia knew he expected his brother to get killed, never considering that he would be in danger just by being related to him.

Eight days later, the funeral was held. Cecilia didn't attend, but was well informed through social media that all the people who had spoken badly about him attended and wept like they cared. His ex-girlfriend made a show of throwing herself in front of everyone in a grand performance of tears that made her eyeliner smear her cheeks in black streaks; she'd coincidentally decided to not wear her usual water-proof eyeliner that day. The older brother and mother watched, his brother likely feeling nervous about standing out in the open while his mother simply watched her son being buried, her grey eyes dry of any tears after days of sobbing. Did she blame her eldest son for his death? Cecilia did, because of him she would have no one to sit with in Calculus the following year. Though she wanted to go to the funeral, her parents discouraged it, horrified that she'd been near that bad seed for almost an entire year.

Instead, she went to the place he'd been shot, a dirty street corner where people had placed a badly printed photo of Thirty-nine. A torn teddy bear holding a heart asking for a valentine sat underneath it, along with several candy wrappers and a half full beer bottle. Smoothing the taped photo over the light pole, Cecilia recognized the image as the one on his high school ID card. It was the first and last image she ever saw of him smiling, and, letting the tears fall, she moved her hand from the image, letting the paper curl at the corners. The single rose she held in her hand didn't seem appropriate for the pathetic roadside memorial, but it was the only way to get it to him. She put the rose in the beer bottle.

Leland Francis Norton: The Making of a Hometown Hero

Alben J. Chamberlain

As a San Bernardino native I grew up just two blocks from the main entry to the Norton Air Force Base. Yet I never knew that until 1950 it had been named the San Bernardino Air Force Base or why the name was changed.

I had spent most of my Junior and Senior High School years worrying about a war in far off Viet Nam and hoping it would end before I graduated and became eligible for the draft.

In my ninth grade year the school secretary at Curtis Junior High School came to our history class to read an exciting and frightening letter from her son who was supposed to be a clerk/typist serving in Viet Nam. When the Tet Offensive broke out in January 1968 her son was placed on a machine gun and sent into combat against the Viet Cong (and NVA dressed as Viet Cong) in the battle to retake the city of Hue. The letter was full of death and destruction but somehow reassuring because at least her son had survived the battle.

The war was still going strong in the second semester of my junior year in high school when a close friend from my sandlot baseball days was killed by a land mine in that now dreaded conflict. Billy Owens was my age but had quit high school at age 16 in order to join the US Marines. His mother had signed the papers and had stated that Billy would be 18 by the time he reached boot camp. I doubt if the recruiter ever looked at his birth certificate.

I remember seeing letters from Billy to his mother whenever I dropped by his house to see what he was up to. Billy was proud to be a Marine and proud to serve his country even if the war was no longer very popular at home. When I attended his closed coffin funeral I tried to console Billy's mother who was completely bereft and grief stricken. I remember that afterwards I had vowed to avoid going to fight in that war no matter what it took.

In my senior year we had a school assignment to research and to write about the life of a local hero of World War II or the war in Korea. My mother suggested that I write about Leland F. Norton since she had worked at the Air Force Base during World War II and still remembered reading about Captain Norton's tragic death in the skies over France. The Air Force Base near our home had been renamed in order to honor his memory and to commemorate his sacrifice.

In my writing assignment I learned that Leland Francis Norton, like me, had been born here in San Bernardino (on March 12, 1921). He had attended Eliot Elementary School, Arrowview Junior High School and graduated from San Bernardino High School in 1939. During these years he would have heard about Japan's vicious assault against China and Germany's annexation of territory in Europe. I wondered then if he had dreaded the onrushing war the way I was dreading the conflict in South-East Asia.

Leland Norton began his college career at San Bernardino Valley Community College. I remember thinking at the time if he had some high school or college sweetheart and plans for a married life once he had finished his education. The official biographies never seem to speak of the affairs of the heart or about future plans interrupted.

What is recorded is that in the fall of 1941 Leland Norton dropped out of his college studies in order to join the Canadian Air Force. Great Britain was barely withstanding the German air assault and was in desperate need of new pilots. With the USA still officially neutral, the only way that a US pilot candidate could join the war effort was through the Canadian Air Force.

Then in March 1942 with the USA now all in with Great Britain in the war against Hitler and Hirohito, Norton transferred over to the US Army Air Force. He was sent first to Maine and then to Greenland where he was in a search and rescue squadron. He could have stayed at this position of relative safety and avoided the horrors of air combat, but that was not the nature of this young man.

He applied for a combat position and was trained to be a bomber pilot in the summer of 1943. By 1944 Leland Norton was the Deputy Commander of the 640th Bombardment Squadron in the United Kingdom. At that time a pilot or crewman on a bomber was expected to fly a minimum of 20 missions before they were released from further bombing missions. Unfortunately only about 1 out of every 5 pilots or crewmen ever passed the twenty mission mark alive and uninjured.

We do not know of the perils or terrors that Captain Leland Norton went through on his first fifteen missions because he never lived to talk about or to write about it. Pilots were not allowed to mention the specifics of their missions in letters home so it is doubtful that Norton's parents knew just how deadly each mission actually was.

On his sixteenth mission on May 27, 1944 his squadron of A-20 Havoc bombers was assigned to attack a German marshaling yard. Captain Norton had just passed his 23rd birthday. The A-20 Havoc that Captain Norton was piloting was struck by German anti-aircraft fire. Knowing that the craft would not make it back to the base Captain Norton ordered his crew to bail out while he remained at the controls as long as possible to ensure that they could parachute to safety.

It is not known whether Captain Norton went down with his bomber near Amiens, France or, as one account claims, Norton parachuted out safely only to be killed when the unreleased bombs on the craft exploded in the crash.

After his tragic death Captain Norton was awarded the Distinguished Flying Cross (DFC), the highest award offered by the US Army Air Force. He was also given the Purple Heart, an award for any soldier who was wounded or killed in the line of duty. The DFC citation was given "for self sacrificing regard for the safety of his crew and fellowmen bringing great distinction on himself and the Army Air Forces."

Captain Norton's death in combat was a major news event here in San Bernardino and throughout Southern California. It must have been a crushing blow to his parents Thomas F. Norton and Vernice Norton who had such high hopes for their brave son. I still remembered how broken Billy Owen's mother seemed at his unexpected funeral when he had just passed his seventeenth birthday. I did my best to console her but she just sobbed that her son should have been in high school with his friends.

In 1950 in a special ceremony, the San Bernardino Air Force Base, then just 8 years old, was renamed Norton Air Force Base in order to honor the memory of hometown hero Captain Leland F. Norton. Captain Norton's remains had been buried at a US military cemetery in France, but in 1952 Norton's parents traveled to France to have his casket removed so it could be reburied in a ceremony at the Mountain View Cemetery in San Bernardino. His remains are marked by a memorial within sight of the San Bernardino Mountains he had grown up seeing as a child and a young adult.

I also attended San Bernardino Community College but unlike Leland F. Norton I did not drop out to fight for my country. I received a very high draft number in the final draft lottery held in 1972 and could not be drafted so all my high school fears went unrealized.

Leland Norton's generation had been labeled as "The Greatest Generation" in a much acclaimed book by that title. What then would my generation be called "The Shirker's Generation or the Reluctant Generation"? Either way I never fought in combat for my country though after earning a BA degree I served as a supply officer in the US Navy Reserve.

I often think about Captain Norton and the legacy he left here in San Bernardino as a hometown war hero. In 2011 long after Norton Air Force Base was closed down and his portrait removed from the wall of the Officer's Club, the San Bernardino City Unified School District broke ground for a new Norton Elementary School. This action assured that his name would not be completely forgotten in the community that shaped this extraordinary hero.

Still Life in San Bernardino
John Bender

Yellow, oblong, bruised brown,
just out of the ice box,
I wonder, pear, how long you're going to be free.
I know you had a scent before refrigeration
You fell from a tree, but my yard doesn't have any trees.
Stem at the top like a chimney
puckered at the bottom as we
all are
Going to take a bite, you know that.
Going to share a taste with our wives
Some kind of crazy knowledge like Eve
and Adam or the ex-con across the street
playing with his kids
for the first time in years
and everyone is laughing and everyone is smiling
and everyone is hoping the fresh thing
is not to get bruised anymore
and the striped scanner label on your back
even if we swallowed
the blue plastic
it would still come back.

Song for San Bernardino
Ruth Nolan

—the pain shall pass, but the beauty will remain—Renoir

I've not gone to confession
since early childhood,
lost to St. Bernardine's Church
in downtown San Bernardino
as I've been for many years
since abandoning
the city of my birth
at the age of 13
trading religion
in the Inland Empire
for the guiltless desert
now, there are
so many canyons
of secrets
to unfold

II

I used to explore
with my brothers and dad
through the fire-singed
cottonwoods along the
Santa Ana River bottom

where ancient waters
from hidden seeps
in the old volcano
named Mt. San Gorgonio
that towers above our town.
During my childhood
we could barely see its peak
through the smog.
Coyote weeps
as the mountain stirs again
so much smoke
in his eyes
so much violence
in the sky
his tears
joining the
River of Lost Souls.

III

I once knew only
Catholic dreams
fueled by Spaniards
spread across the land
with the blood of American Indians
crosses everywhere
the 18th century asistencia in Redlands

that stands to this day
next to a mental hospital
the rise of Catholics and Mormons
and Anglo-European
ways, on and on,
the blood shed then and now
San Bernardino
forgotten city of dreams
forsaken city of Hells Angels
the first McDonalds on "E" Street
the Rolling Stones at Swing Auditorium
the All-American City
situated where fault zones meet
where the arrowhead points down
to my hometown
flowing and overflowing
with the blood
of all the world
of all the old, secret stories
buried, untold
there's so much to excavate
from beneath
this toxic river, buried as it is now
by freeway overpasses, exploited
by irritating helicopters,
news cameras
the Internet
the world

hovers above our town
SWAT teams
are on the way
but chemicals and bullets
and religious ideologies
gone mad
erupting in our town
haunting us
with their forever
half – lives.
Silent Night
is our love song
this season, and
the cycles of our river
goes on and on
harmonizing
flood and drought
the rise and fall
Christmas decorations
in the conference hall
lose their shine
guiltless people
lose their lives
when religion
isn't enough
when religion
weighs too much

IV

December
is fat
this year
gentle snow
on the mountains
deep shadows
in the foothills
cars on the rivers of freeways
flowing day and night
from the mountains
through our suffering
to the promising sea
I believe that the Virgin Mary
I once loved and knew
outside the confessional booth
at St. Bernardine's Church
is still painted blue.

*(in memory of the victims of the San Bernardino terrorist
shooting on Dec. 2, 2015)*

Growing Air
Sant Khalsa

Growing Air focuses on an expansive forest of approximately one thousand ponderosa pine trees I planted during Spring 1992 as part of the effort to reforest Holcomb Valley (clear-cut by settlers during the Southern California gold rush of 1860) and improve air quality in the Inland Empire. My project is primarily photo-based works that derive from my response to this most personal yet public space and an in-depth field investigation into the natural and cultural history of this unique and complex landscape located in the San Bernardino National Forest.

In 1992, I was invited to produce new work for the thematic group exhibition *Smog: A Matter of Life and Breath* curated by Kim Abeles for the California Museum of Photography at the University of California, Riverside (UCR). The Los Angeles basin and more specifically the inland region of Riverside and San Bernardino have long suffered from the worst air quality in the U.S. due to a large population, car culture and factories as well as sunny, stagnant weather and a bowl-like topography, and more recently forest fires due to drought. The region has the highest level of ozone pollution and second worst for year-round particulates in the nation.

Each artist in *Smog* was paired with research faculty at the UCR Air Pollution Research Center. During a meeting with my collaborating scientist, Paul Miller, I asked "what was the best thing I could do as an individual to positively impact air quality in the Inland Empire?" He said "plant trees." I planted hundreds of ponderosa pine seedlings as a volunteer with the National Forest Service in Holcomb Valley north of Big Bear Lake during the 1992 spring planting season. Also, on May 1, 1992 (during the Rodney

King riots in South Central Los Angeles), four of my New Genres class students, Ross Chambers, D'Arcy Curwen, Michael Morehead and Melissa Prado joined me and each planted one hundred ponderosa pine seedlings. (Native ponderosa pine was selected, propagated and germinated locally because of its resilience to fire.) My planting experiences were physically labor intensive yet emotionally profound and cognitively transformative; inspiring the creation of the site-specific installation "The Sacred Breath" and photo wall installation, "S.O.S.: We are killing trees, therefore we are killing ourselves" for the *Smog* exhibition. Many of my subsequent photo, sculptural and installation works related to trees, forests, air quality and watersheds over the past two decades evolved from the planting experiences and these artworks.

I returned to the site of the seedling plantings for the first time twenty-five years later, to find an extraordinarily beautiful and healthy forest of 6-8 inch diameter, 30-40 foot high pine trees. The forest is producing oxygen needed for us to breathe over our lifetimes as well as storing and using carbon to offset our carbon footprint. While there, I saw many species of birds and wildlife, and people experiencing the forest as a site for individual reflection and family interactions.

Since celebrating the 25th anniversary of the trees' plantings, I have been spending time in the forest, developing a meaningful connection, conducting creative research and producing new works. My interest is with both the micro and macro aspects of the forest site: what is seen and unseen; historical, scientific and spiritual; and personal and global. As in many of my works, the essential life elements of air, water, fire and earth play a significant role in expressing the symbiotic relationship between the natural world and myself (and all humanity). My intention is to create artworks that express an intimate association with the forest, grounded in our life-sustaining connection with the trees.

My philosophy as an artist is founded in the belief that individual and societal evolution comes from deep and meaningful conscious raising experiences. My artworks are intended to spark the realization that we are nature and initiate change in human action. My works are both personal and social-political in nature. Photographing is an integral part of my art and meditative practice of mindful observation. It is a means to visually organize and make sense of what I often perceive as a chaotic, conflicted and complex world. My perspective is expressed through a photographic style that encompasses the documentary, interpretive and subjective.

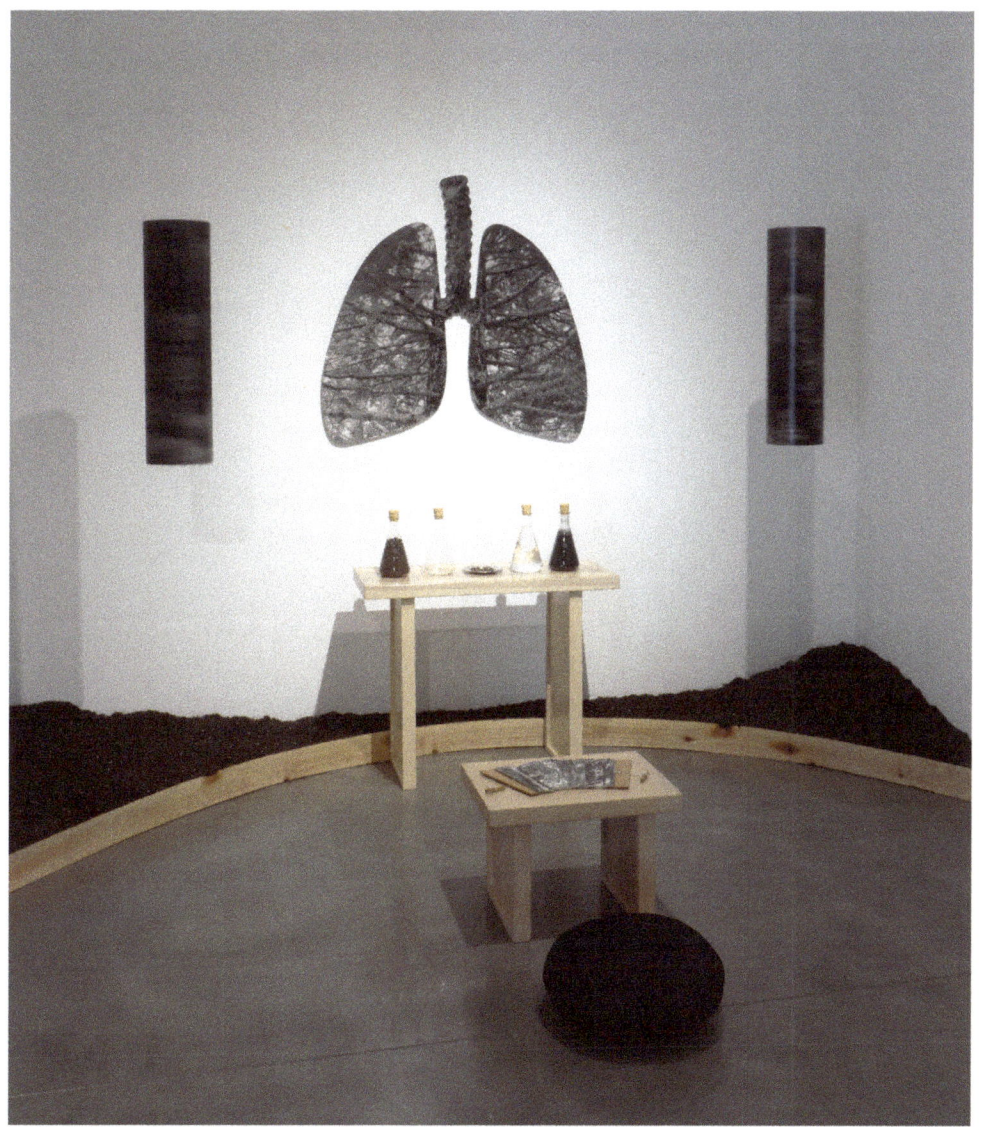

The Sacred Breath, 1992
Installation at MOAH Lancaster, 2018

The Sacred Breath (Prayer Book), 1992
Gelatin silver prints, wood and string

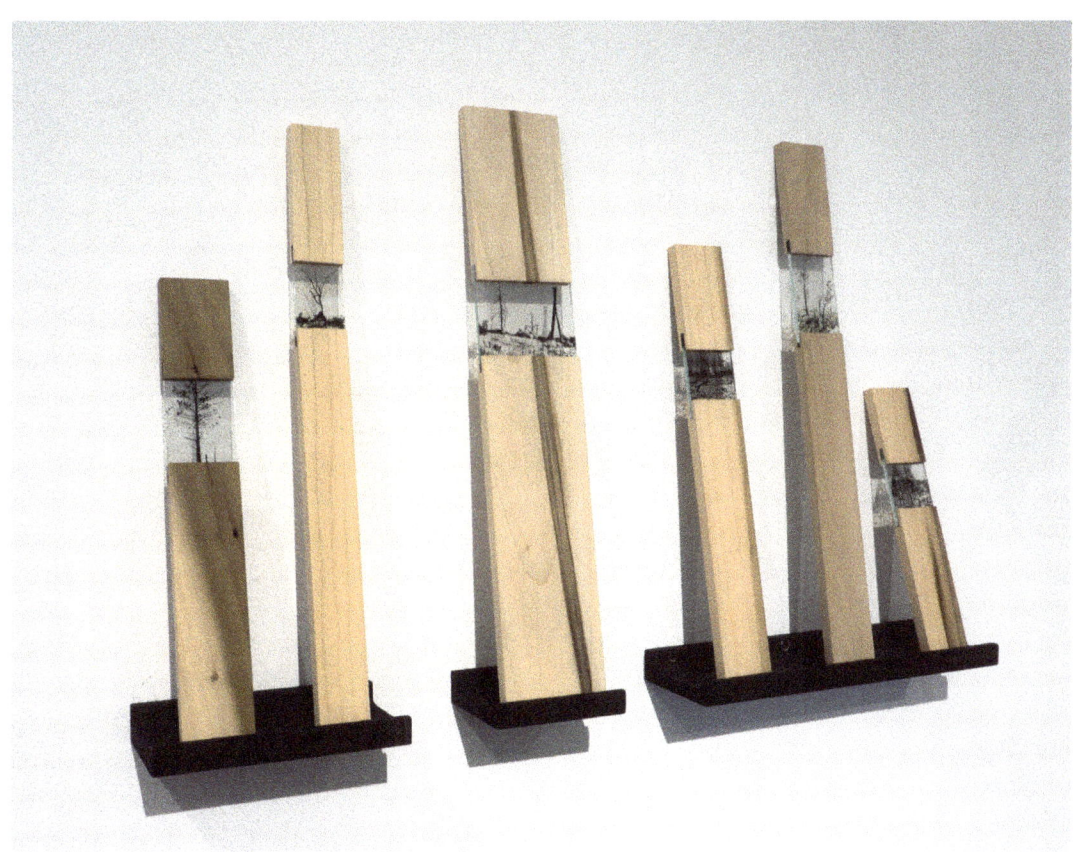

Trees and Seedlings, 2000-2018
Gelatin silver transparencies, wood and glass

Holcomb Valley (Ponderosa pines planted in 1992), 2017
Archival pigment print

Holcomb Valley (Remains from 1860's gold rush and Ponderosa pines planted in 1992), 2017, Archival pigment print

Holcomb Valley (Ponderosa pines planted in 1992), 2017
Archival pigment print

Holcomb Valley (Pulverized Gold Ore), 2017
Archival pigment print

Holcomb Valley (Ponderosa pines planted in gold tailings in 1992), 2017
Archival pigment print

Holcomb Valley (Ponderosa pines planted in 1992), 2017
Archival pigment print

Holcomb Valley (Ponderosa pines planted in 1992 with old growth stump), 2017
Archival pigment print

SAN BERNARDINO, SINGING

Youth Writing

Creativity as a Learning Lens: An Introduction to S.C.I.P.P. Work

Allyson Jeffredo

At California State University San Bernardino (CSUSB), I was fortunate enough to take a class informally called S.C.I.P.P.—Students and Coyotes Instruction in Poetry and Prose. It is a class dedicated to pedagogy, essentially a class designed to teach the methodology and practice of teaching creative writing to children to promote a positive environment around literacy, created by Juan Delgado, CSUSB Professor of English, Will Beshears and Larry Light, both Master Teachers at Manuel S. Salinas Creative Arts Elementary School. This class continues to be held on the CSUSB campus where the Salinas Elementary School students and their families visit to bridge the distance between institutions of education. In the class, the students experience a positive literacy environment on the university campus, while the parents are given information on how to ensure their students not only graduate high school, but also attend post-secondary institutions like CSUSB.

This is where I realized the power of words. Someone can manipulate, empower, disempower, enlighten, or destroy a person in a single sentence, and each of these can occur simultaneously in an individual paragraph or entire essay. Never once have I felt more reverence to words than after working with the students of the Inland Empire and beyond, especially the students of Manuel S. Salinas Creative Arts Elementary School found in Muscoy, a section of San Bernardino that has yet to be fully inculcated by urbanization. Where men wrestle with wild horses in their front lawns, and students come to school the day after a family member was murdered on that same green earth.

***

In our society, we do not respect the child. We look at children as lesser, inadequate versions of adults, which is so distant from the truth it seems outrageous. Children are people who respect honesty and understanding as much as any other individual. This is not to say children should experience everything an adult does, but it is a great disservice to them when we believe they are unobservant and incapable of complex thought. The only thing really separating children and adults is the level of understanding. In this, I am guilty of underestimating children as well. In many ways, their malleable minds are far more superior to our lineated adult brains. The ways they can leap and stretch and adapt and learn far exceeds the minds of many adults.

In this vein, I am happy and grateful to introduce the writing and artwork of the students from Will Beshears' 4th/5th grade class. In the words of Beshears:

"[This] class is a writing class as part of our 4/5th grade rotation model. We rotate them so they can be better leveled. Traditionally, the biggest restriction to learning is the limitations by age and learning needs of the classroom…So, [this] class is a very advanced reading/writing group…In short, [these classes are designed to ensure the students] don't fall through the cracks—many advanced learners, at least in San Bernardino, are among the most at risk, and disproportionately represent behavioral issues and drop outs."

My Home City
Elizabeth Lorrabaquio

I might live in a home you call strange.

I might live in a home you call weird.

I might even live in a home you call dangerous.

But what is this home?
San Bernardino.

I can't really tell you my favorite place in this beautiful city.

But I can tell you this…

There are many public pools to swim in at summer.

There are lovely homes to keep shelter in the winter.

There are many beautiful flowers and other plants in spring.

And there are even great grocery stores to buy food for holidays in fall.

Not to mention we have lots of fun places to go any day!

I know this might sound like some kind of silly ad to make people

come to a silly place that sounds like heaven, but, the truth is if

you want a beautiful city, come here.

My home. My city.

And I live in a city we call perfect.

I live in a city we call unique.

I live in a city we call safe.

I live in San Bernardino.

Do you?

My Mind
Alaya Delgado

My favorite place in San Bernardino is my mind

My favorite place for many reasons

I can imagine anything like people who look like pancakes

I can imagine what my mind smells like

And right now my mind smells like cheese burgers

My mind is my favorite place because it is like a diary

That no one can see and it is like my map of the world

That I can always remember

My mind is my favorite place because I can do

Whatever I want like pretend to go to sleep at 1 am

Or eating dessert and then lunch I love my mind and

That's one of the things I love about San Bernardino

San Bernardino
Casandra Perez

m
a
y
1
1
2
0
1
7

My room
Is a wonderful place
Full of laughter. It
Feels like a silk blanket.

My room sounds like Wind blowing right Past. When I go
inside I see animals and family there. When you go there,
it will smell Like a pink daisy in a forest. When you look
at it you will be happy like you just won a medal.

My Mind
Edward Walsh

Whenever I'm bored, I think of school,
When I think of school, I think of my best friend Nic,
In my friends, I see my classmates,
In my classmates, I see classrooms.

In all those classrooms, I see my grandma's house.
In my grandma's house, I see my PS4
In the consoles, I see Need for Speed Rivals.
In my games, I see me.
In me, I see my favorite place.

The place I've been the whole time,
My head.

My Favorite Place in San Bernardino
Juliana Almazan

My favorite place in San Bernardino is the movie theater. I love the theater because I love the new movies and the adventures.

One day my mom told everyone that she wanted to go to the movies. So they started talking about what movie, how many people, and who was going to take care of the babies. When that was happening Valerie (the 4-year-old) started shooting us with the water gun that she was playing outside (it was really hot). Then, after we all changed, we got into the car to go to the movie theater.

When we were getting out of the car, my uncle surprised us with paying for all of the tickets, so the adults were really happy that they got out of the house. We got the tickets but when were walking inside the lady told us we had to wait outside in a line for the watching Finding Dory because it was the first day anybody saw it. So some of us stayed at the line while the rest of us went to get snacks. Everyone got popcorn and drinks. My uncle got a hamburger and my other crazy uncle got nachos, popcorn, soda, ice cream, and skittles. I got a small Icee, but it looked more like a large. When I saw the large, I knew mine was a small. When all of us went back to the line, a minute after they told us to go in, and I was not focusing where I was going and I hit my head in the post and everyone was laughing even the people in the back.

We were inside the room and watching Finding Dory when I had to use the restroom and I went and the movie was finished. I had an awesome time at the movies.

Favorite Place In San Bernardino
Rubi Salazar

San Bernardino,What a beautiful place,
Full of everything,
But I rarely go out,
Because of the family and I,
Since there is too many of us.
So why bother right,
There is too many opportunities,
That I could NOT go to.
But there is only my mind,
My fun place,
Where I could never get bored.
My mind is where I could do everything,
Where I could not get disturbed,
Where I'm calm,
Where everything happens,
And mostly where I am
Doing things I have never done.
This place is great,
It is fun,
No problems,
The opposite of the real world.
What everyone would wish for.

Youth
Sophia Fuentes

Age...
A black hole which there is no escape,
you just fall
      fall
            fall
Youth, just like a racecar
one moment here, the next...
gone.

Time drains all youth the from you.
Once a lively rose,
now a wilted one
youth is broken promises,
mistakes,
cold hearts.

You become a broken machine,
one that has been thrown away.
One that burns to the touch,
leaving a painful scar.

Youth will always leave you,
no matter what.

San Bernardino

Vanesa Valero

The light of my life.
That rainbow of hope.
That fantasy that
came to life. That fantasy of a
perfect life. That fantasy
that smells like
joy. That fantasy That fantasy
that brought that splash of
Joy. That fantasy that
brought me the unicorn
I hug when I am scared.

Scared of the demons
Waiting to escape. That black ink
with blood eyes, stabbing and
picking at me. Scared of the nightmare this fantasy
is covering. That nightmare with
a fog. A fog that blinds you
from the truth. The truth that has been covered
like a present. The truth of the evil around
us. The evil that has fear misery and

Death.

My Mind
Elizabeth Martinez

San Bernardino is the perfect place to visit. My favorite place in San Bernardino is my mind. My mind helps me think when I am frustrated, I close my eyes and start to think. I imagine crazy stuff in my mind when I am hungry, like me being a hamburger. When I am taking a test, I try to not think of other stuff that would get me distracted, like me getting nervous when a teacher calls me to go to his classroom. I love to be in my mind a lot, like when I am sleeping I try to think how I look like when I am older and me getting good grades and being a great dancer. Every time I think of something scary, I tell my mom and she always tells me everything is going to be fine. I get used to my mind a lot, I feel safe in my mind than what I feel in my real life. I think of many people in my mind that I see in school, like my friends and my best friend and, most of all, my family. People also think that their mind is their favorite place in San Bernardino like my best friend, Alaya. She is always there for me, that is why I think of her as my sister, even if I already have a sister. My mind is always going to be my favorite place and nobody can take it away from me. I can always think of my mind being my real life even if I already have a real life. Every time I am mad or sad I can always put my head down and go to my mind and think, " What should I do?" In my mind, I sometimes see the stuff happening in my real life when I think about it too hard. My mind is my favorite place in San Bernardino.

Art Book
Virinia Torres

A unique place in San Bernardino and it's mine. I have improved and it is the reason I made friends. Addiction is what I call it. It calms me, relieves my stress. It's my friend helping me through tough times. I will never stop my artwork. It's my *dream* to become an artist ever since I was small. My art book keeps me sane. The best place in San Bernardino....they think big and extravagant, yet it's right in my hands small and full, neat and clean.

This is the best you'll get the best place Art.

About *San Bernardino, Singing*

Biographies

TRISTAN ACKER is a San Bernardino based writer/musician. You can catch his solo music as Tanjint Wiggy, his nerdcore hip-hop groups West Coast Avengers and Guardians of the I.E. at westcoastavengers.com and all major streaming services. He writes about rap at ZusEntertainment.com, Nerd culture at NightswithWaifu.com and the Inland Empire at Jooseboxx.com.

KATHLEEN ALCALÁ is the author of six books including "Mrs. Vargas and the Dead Naturalist" and "Spirits of the Ordinary," which was awarded first place in the International Latino Book Awards Books into Movies category. A recipient of the Governors Writers Award in Washington State, two Artist Trust Fellowships, and the Western States Book Award, Kathleen's most recent book is "The Deepest Roots: Finding Food and Community on a Pacific Northwest Island." Kathleen has previous work in Inlandia anthologies, including *Orangelandia: The Literature of Inland Citrus*, edited by Gayle Brandeis. Born in Compton and raised in San Bernardino, Kathleen lives and teaches creative writing in the Northwest.

CYNTHIA ANDERSON lives in the Mojave Desert near Joshua Tree National Park. Her poems have appeared in journals such as *Spillway, Crab Creek Review, Apercus, Askew, San Pedro River Review, Mojave River Review, The Coil,* and *Split Rock Review.* Her work has been nominated for Best of the Net and the Pushcart Prize. She is the author of nine poetry collections and co-editor of the anthology *A Bird Black As the Sun: California Poets on Crows & Ravens.* www.cynthiaandersonpoet.com

ERIKA AYÓN emigrated from Mexico when she was five years old and grew up in South Central Los Angeles. She graduated from UCLA with a B.A. in English. She was selected as a 2009 PEN Emerging Voices Fellow. She has taught poetry to middle and high school students across Los Angeles. Her work has appeared in *The Acentos Review, Chiricú Journal, Orangelandia Anthology, Wide Awake Anthology, Coiled Serpent Anthology*, and elsewhere. Her debut poetry collection *Orange Lady* was published by World Stage Press.

ROSE BALDWIN is a retired civil servant who has learned how to draw sucre from the desert. Since moving from Wisconsin to the Palm Springs area she has published two books: *The Claire Stories,* a collection of short stories about the woman she aspires to be; and *Mike's Magic Burgers* a novel about change, set in a restaurant where the food is magic, and the cool people hang out. Her short stories and poems have appeared in several literary magazines. She is currently working on *Claire and Her Friends* which will be published this summer.

JOHN BENDER is an Inland Empire poet and musician who performs under many different names, including Brutusaurus Rex Chieftain, Bombastus and Henry Heaven. He is CEO and president of Inlandia Institute and co-founder of the poetry performance troupe, Poets in Distress. His latest books include *Brutus in Benderland* and *Tales of an American Peasant.*

MICHELLE BRACKEN is a former elementary school teacher. She's a 2019 fellowship winner at *theOFFICE* and a past participant of the Squaw Valley Community of Writers and the ZYZZYVA Writers' Workshop. Her writing has appeared in Litro UK, the Baltimore Review, Forklift Ohio, The Superstition Review, Empty Mirror, The Coachella Review, and elsewhere.

GAYLE BRANDEIS is the author, most recently, of the novel in poems, *Many Restless Concerns: The Victims of Countess Bathory Speak in*

Chorus (A Testimony), the memoir *The Art of Misdiagnosis* (Beacon Press), and the poetry collection *The Selfless Bliss of the Body* (Finishing Line Press). Earlier books include *Fruitflesh: Seeds of Inspiration for Women Who Write* (HarperOne) and the novels *The Book of Dead Birds* (HarperCollins), which won the Bellwether Prize for Fiction of Social Engagement judged by Barbara Kingsolver, Toni Morrison, and Maxine Hong Kingston, *Self Storage* (Ballantine), *Delta Girls* (Ballantine), and *My Life with the Lincolns* (Henry Holt BYR), which was chosen as a state-wide read in Wisconsin. Her poetry, essays, and short fiction have been widely published in places such as *The New York Times, The Washington Post, O (The Oprah Magazine), The Rumpus, Salon, Longreads*, and more, and have received numerous honors, including a Barbara Mandigo Kelly Peace Poetry Award, Notable Essays in *Best American Essays* 2016 and 2019, the *QPB/Story Magazine* Short Story Award and the 2018 Multi Genre Maverick Writer Award. She served as Inlandia Literary Laureate from 2012-2014 and currently teaches at Sierra Nevada College and Antioch University Los Angeles.

CELENADIANA BUMPUS is the founder of Islands For Writers Publishing. Since 2010, Ms. Bumpus has taught three free creative writing classes year-round every Tuesday at the Janet Goeske Senior Center in Riverside. Ms. Bumpus is the published author of the poetry collection, *Confessions* (1998, The Inevitable Press). Her personal essay was published in *Street Lit: Representing the Urban Landscape* (2014, Scarecrow Press). Her poetry, prose, short stories and short memoir have appeared in the following publications: *Writing From Inlandia* (2012-2019 editions, Inlandia Institute), *Verse/Chorus: A Call and Response Anthology* (2013, Scarecrow Press), *Invisible Memoirs* (2014, Memoir Journal), *Orangelandia: The Literature of Inlandia Citrus* (2014, Inlandia Institute), *Pen 2 Paper Online Journal* (2014), *On The Rusk magazine* (2015), and the *Chameleons Anthology* (2018, Islands For Writers).

ALIX CARMONA is a writer born and raised in Southern California, where she still resides. She is currently finishing her BA is Sociology at California Polytechnic University, Pomona. She continues to write and dedicates her time to continuing her education, as well as, working and reading.

ALBEN CHAMBERLAIN was born in San Bernardino, California on May 22, 1953. He has lived in the Inland Empire for most of his life. He attended San Bernardino Valley College, and received a BA degree from BYU-Hawaii. He earned an MBA from The American Graduate School in Glendale, Arizona as well as several teaching credentials from The University of California-Riverside.

NIKIA CHANEY, Inlandia Literary Laureate (2016-2018), is the author of *Us, Mouth* (University of Hell Press, 2018), winner of the Marsh Hawk Robert Creeley Award in 2015, as well as two chapbooks, *Sis Fuss* (2012, Orange Monkey Publishing) and *ladies, please* (2012, Dancing Girl Press). Her poetry was chosen by Nikki Giovanni as the winner of the 2012 OSA Enizagam Poetry Award. She has received fellowships and grants from Cave Canem, the Millay Colony for the Arts, Squaw Valley, and the Barbara Demings Fund for Women. She is founding editor of *shufpoetry*, an online journal for experimental poetry, and founding editor of Jamii Publishing, a publishing imprint dedicated to fostering community among poets and writers.Nikia holds two MFAs, one from Antioch University, Los Angeles, and one from California State University, San Bernardino. Her work has been published in *Iowa Review, Portland Review, Saranac Review, 491, Pearl, Sugar House Review, Welter, Blackberry Magazine, Badlands*, and elsewhere.

CHRISTINE CHATTERTON M.ED. is an author, artist, poet, photographer. She received her B.S. in Geology from Michigan State University in 1976 and her Masters in Education and Reading Specialization from

Northern Arizona University in 1987. She is a retired special education teacher and a reading improvement specialist in California for almost thirty years. She is the author of *Courage of the Heart: An American Odyssey 1915 to 1923*, a true historical narrative and love story of World War I based on war letters from her husband's grandparents. Other publications include the children's book *Samuel's Alphabet Zoo*, and a humorous memoir of growing up near Detroit, *The Kids on Ford Street*.

MICAH CHATTERTON'S first collection, *Go to the Living*, was published by Inlandia Books in 2017. His work is forthcoming or has appeared in *EcoTheo*, *Best New Poets 2013*, *B O D Y*, *Tupelo Quarterly*, *Ruminate*, *LETTERS*, and *Slice*. He lives and teaches writing in the Inland Empire region of southern California.

Retired from part-time work as an editor/proofreader, SYLVIA CLARKE is enjoying a slower life, catching up a bit on reading and doing a bit more writing. She and her husband Wil spend most of their time together at home, going to appointments, or out walking Katie, their dog, in the fields near their home.

WIL CLARKE has lived in the Inland Empire for 34 years. He published an article in the *San Bernardino Sun* some years ago. For many years he lived in Africa both as a child of missionaries and as a missionary with his wife. He is currently writing a memoir.

DEENAZ COACHBUILDER is a writer, visual artist and environmental advocate. She was an administrator in the Special Education Department, and then principal of Anderson School, in the San Bernardino Unified School District, for many years. Anderson School was attended by students with profound and severe disabilities, and pupils in the Community Day School Program. Her poetry, commentaries, essays and book reviews have been published internationally. Deenaz' books of poems, *Metal Horse and Shadows: A Soul's Journey (2019),* and *Imperfect Fragments (2014),* have been received with critical acclaim in the U.S. and abroad. She is the recipient of several recognitions, including President Obama's Volunteer Service Award. Deenaz is a board member of literary and environmental organizations, and stays involved in community associations.

CARLOS E. CORTÉS is the Edward A. Dickson Emeritus Professor of History at the University of California, Riverside. His books include his memoir, Rose Hill: An Intermarriage before Its Time (Heyday) and a book of poetry, Fourth Quarter: Reflections of a Cranky Old Man (Bad Knee Press), which received honorable mention in the 2017 International Latino Book Awards. Cortés served as the Creative/Cultural Advisor for Nickelodeon's "Dora the Explorer" and "Go, Diego, Go!," for which he received the 2009 NAACP Image Award. He also performs his one-person autobiographical play, A Conversation with Alana: One Boy's Multicultural Rite of Passage.

JUAN DELGADO is Professor Emeritus in the English Department at California State University, San Bernardino, where he chaired the English and Communication Studies Departments. His collections of poetry include *Green Web* (1994) published by the University of Georgia Press and was selected by poet Dara Weir for the Contemporary Poetry Prize; *El Campo* (1998) published by Capra Press and was a collaboration with the Chicano painter Simon Silva; *Rush of Hands* (2003) was published by the University of Arizona Press. His most recent book, *Vital Signs* (2013), was a collaboration with photographer Thomas McGovern and won the American Book Award given by the Before Columbus Foundation. In recent years, he has presented his photopoetics and signage in museum exhibitions throughout southern California such as *Más Allá del los Fences* at the Peppers Gallery in Redlands, 2017. *Manos, Espaldas y Blossoms*, a collaborative art project with Thomas McGovern that featured their artwork in the groves of California Citrus State Historical Park, 2018. *Sign Language*, a mixed media exhibition at the CSUH Art Galleries, featured the collaborative work of Thomas McGovern and Juan Delgado, and the artwork of Amando Lerma and Carlos Ramirez, aka "The Date Farmers."

SHEELA SITARAM FREE was born in Mumbai, India and has spent equal halves of her life in India and in America. Her B.A. in English Literature and Language, M.A. in English and American Literature and Language, M.A. in Hindi, Ph.D. in the Contemporary American Novel-novels of John Updike-and her twenty four years of teaching all across the United States in Universities, colleges, and community colleges reveal her life-long passion for the power of words. Her collection of poetry entitled Of Fractured Clocks, Bones and Windshields was published by Plain View Press in February 2009. She has been writing for over 20 years but it was the Inland Empire that inspired/motivated her to publish and she has simply loved being a part of it for 9 years now and she draws on a great deal of material from it in her poetry.

NAN FRIEDLEY is a retired special education teacher and graduate of Ball State University, Muncie, IN. Her writings have been published in a poetry chapbook, "Short Bus Ride" by Bad Knee Press, Indiana Voice Journal, Inlandia Anthologies, and "Three" a nonfiction anthology collection by Push Pen Press. Nan participates in the Riverside Inlandia Workshop.

JEREMIAH GILBERT is an award-winning photographer and avid traveler based out of Southern California. He likes to travel light and shoot hand-held. His travels have taken him to over eighty countries spread across six continents. His photography has been published internationally, in both digital and print publications, and has been exhibited worldwide. He was born in San Bernardino, was a professor at San Bernardino Valley College for twenty years, and now serves as an Executive Director at the San Bernardino Community College District. His photography can be found on Instagram @jg_travels

ALEXIS GONZALEZ is an up and coming author, blogger, and inspirational speaker. She is the founder of www.vibratetocreate.com, where she writes inspirational pieces—with the intention to uplift and empower others. Alexis has an innate passion to help others to seek to find the beauty in all situations of their lives, and this is evident in the creative pursuits she embarks on. In her work, she shares personal experiences and self-reflections in the hopes of assisting others in doing the same in their own lives.

liz gonzález grew up in the San Bernardino Valley. She's the author of *Dancing in the Santa Ana Winds: Poems y Cuentos New and Selected* (Los Nietos Press 2018). Her poetry, fiction, and creative nonfiction have been published widely and appeared in or will soon appear in *Puro Chicanx Writers of the 21st Century, Voices de la Luna: A Quarterly Literature & Arts Magazine, Fire and Rain: Ecopoetry of California*, and *Voices from Leimert Park Redux: Los Angeles Poetry Anthology*. She was recently featured on Latinopia.com, KUCR's Radio Aztlan, and KPCC's Unheard L.A. For more about liz: lizgonzalez.com

MICHELLE GONZALEZ grew up in San Bernardino and moved to Riverside at the age of three. She earned her MFA in creative writing from National University in 2010. Since then she has participated in various Inlandia workshops and events. Michelle has also published four chapbooks including, *Morning in the House by the Field, Afternoon in the Park by the Lake, Evening in the House by the Field*, and *Wild Chrysanthemum*. She has also lead writing workshops in the local area.

Cindy Bousquet Harris is a poet, photographer, licensed marriage and family therapist, and the editor of *Spirit Fire Review*. Her poems can be found in, or forthcoming from, *Nostos, Pomona Valley Review, Unlost Journal, Inlandia: A Literary Journey*, and in several anthologies. She's lead poetry workshops for adults and at-risk youth. Her book manuscript, Ice in Heaven, was a finalist for the 2018 Hillary Gravendyk Prize. She lives in Southern California's Inland Empire with her husband and their children. You can reach her at: SpiritFireReview2@gmail.com

Allyson Jeffredo is a poet, writer and educator from the Coachella Valley. She currently runs the reading and writing performs for libraries throughout Riverside County. Her work can be found in places like Entropy and Lunch Ticket among others. Find out more at https://www.allysonjeffredo.com/.

Sant Khalsa is an artist, educator and activist whose artworks are widely exhibited, published and acquired by museums including the Los Angeles County Museum of Art, Nevada Museum of Art and Center for Creative Photography in Tucson. Khalsa has been awarded fellowships and grants from the National Endowment for the Arts, California Arts Council, California Council for the Humanities and was the inaugural recipient of the Society for Photographic Education *Insight Award* for her significant contributions to the field of photography. She is a Professor of Art, Emerita at California State University, San Bernardino and lives in Joshua Tree.

Katherine Cech Latonio (Kay) moved to San Bernardino in 1970 at the age of twelve and lived in the Inland Empire until 2018 when she retired and relocated to Humboldt County north of the "Redwood Curtain." She enjoys writing poetry and stories that are often connected to geographical place and has been pondering how place can affect both individuals and communities. She has had her poetry published in various small publications and has performed spoken word pieces at a number of events.

CASANDRA LÓPEZ is a California Indian (Cahuilla/Tongva/Luiseño) and Chicana writer who has received support from *CantoMundo, Bread Loaf,* and *Tin House.* She's the author of the poetry collection, *Brother Bullet* and has been selected for residencies with the School of Advanced Research, Storyknife, Hedgebrook and Headlands Center for the Arts. Her memoir-in-progress, *A Few Notes on Grief* was granted a 2019 James W. Ray Venture Project Award. She's a founding editor of *As/Us* and teaches at Northwest Indian College.

JAMES LUNA was born and grew up in San Bernardino. He is the author of four children's books: *The Runaway Piggy/El Cochinito Fugitivo, A Mummy in Her Backpack/Una momia en su mochila, The Place Where You Live/El lugar donde vives* and *Growing Up on the Playground/ Nuestro patio de recreo,* all published by Piñata Books, Arte Público Press. *Piggy* was awarded the 2012 Tejas Star Award as chosen by the students of the Rio Grande Valley of Texas. He has participated in panels and readings at the Texas Book Festival, the Latino Book and Family Festival and the California Association for Bilingual Education conference. His school presentations have included schools in Southern California and Texas. He holds an MFA in Fiction Writing from National University and is a member of SCBWI. His author website is moonstories.com. He contributes to the Rhubarbs Writing Group blog at http://www.rhubarbwg.com/, and has his own blog at https:// cookteachwritedaddy.wordpress.com/. He currently teaches sixth grade at Madison Elementary School, in Riverside, where he has taught grades 3, 5 and 6 for over 30 years. He and his wife live in Riverside.

JUANITA E. MANTZ ("JEM") is a writer, performer and lawyer/deputy public defender in Riverside representing those incompetent to stand trial. Her stories have been published in numerous literary journals including The Acentos Review, As/Us, Muse, The James Franco Review and Inlandia Journal, amongst others. JEM is a member of the Macondo Writers Workshop and a VONA alum. She recently completed her memoir, "My Inland Empire", about growing up in Ontario, California in the 1970s and 1980s. You can read her blog about her life at `http://wwwlifeofjemcom-jemmantz.blogspot.com`. JEM has presented at AWP, the UCR Punk Conference and she was a 2016 cast member of "Listen to Your Mother" Burbank. She is a proud resident of San Bernardino and loves punk rock music.

ADAM DANIEL MARTINEZ first scraped his knee playing in his hometown of San Bernardino, California. Since then, as a first-generation Chicano college student, he has earned a dual MA/MFA in English and Creative Writing at Chapman University. Adam has written and performed music in the Inland Empire for over 15 years, most notably under the moniker Faimkills. He is the co-founder of *Pour Vida*, a digital literary zine. Currently, Adam enjoys sharing his love for words with his students as an English professor at Chaffey College. He lives in Redlands, California with his wife and two cats, Virginia and Percival. His manuscript, *Remyth: A Postmodernist Ritual*, won the 2019 regional Hillary Gravendyk Prize and is forthcoming.

NICOLE MCDONALD graduated in 2018 from the University of Redlands. She is a native of the Inland Empire. She has lived many places including Brooklyn, Chicago, Dallas, London, Montreal, and San Diego, but the Inland Empire is home.

THOMAS MCGOVERN is a photographer, writer and educator. He is the author of *Bearing Witness (to AIDS)*, *HARD BOYS + BAD GIRLS*, *Amaz-*

ing Grace, and co-author with poet Juan Delgado of *Vital Signs* which received an American Book Award in 2014. His photographs are in the permanent collections of The International Center of Photography, Los Angeles County Museum of Art, Brooklyn Museum of Art, Baltimore Museum of Art, Museum of Fine Arts Houston, Schomburg Center for Research in Black Culture, and Riverside Art Museum, among others. His exhibition reviews and features have appeared in *Afterimage*, *Art-week*, *Art Papers* and *Art Issues* and he is the founder and editor-in-chief of *Dotphotozine*. He is a professor of art at California State University, San Bernardino.

RORY MURRAY is an artist, activist, singer/songwriter, muralist and proud San Bernardino resident. Credits include illustration for Carol Wright's book for children, *Roselle's Cooking Again!*, and Patricia Sach's *Stan the Spray Can*. Recent work can be seen at the Wigwam Motel on Route 66 and The Living Mural, which surrounds the McDonalds Museum. While painting this mural, he greeted many visitors from around the world. They flock to see the true and humble beginnings of Dick & Mac McDonald. The love and support for and from our community following the tragedy of December 2, 2015 inspired him to write a Love Song for San Bernardino. It's called WE WILL RISE and is available on YouTube or for downloaded at CD Baby.

RUTH NOLAN was born in San Bernardino and grew up in the Mojave Desert town of Apple Valley. A former wildland firefighter for the BLM and USFS, she is a longtime professor of English, CA desert studies and creative writing at College of the Desert. Ruth is also co-founder of the first Inlandia Writers Workshop in Riverside and editor of *No Place for a Puritan: the Literature of California's Deserts* (Heyday) and coeditor of *Fire and Rain: Ecopoetry of California*. She has contributed writing to *McSweeney's*; *Women's Studies Quarterly*; KCET *LA Artbound* and *Tending Nature* series; the *Desert Sun/USA Today*; *Desert Oracle*;

The LA Fiction Anthology (Red Hen Press); *She Explores*; the *LA Times*; *News from Native California* and more. Her new poetry book *Ghost Flower* is forthcoming from Yak Press this spring.

KEENAN NORRIS'S novel *Brother and the Dancer* won the 2012 James D. Houston Award and was nominated for the inaugural John Leonard Prize. His chapbook *By the Lemon Tree* was nominated for the 2019 California Book Award. He is also the editor of the critical volume *Street Lit: Representing the Urban Landscape*. His short fiction appears in several literary journals, as well as the anthologies *Oakland Noir, Inlandia: A Journey Through the Literature of Southern California's Inland Empire* and *Post-Soul Satire: Black Identity after Civil Rights*. His novella *Lustre* will be published by Goliad Press in 2020. Keenan has also published journalism, editorials and academic scholarship. In popmatters.com, his work has explored Oakland's relationship to Silicon Valley, as well as the exploitation of Black Studies programs by university athletic departments. He has published "Post-Mortem Morning: Oakland and the Remains of the Left" and "Ben Carson, Thug Life and Malcolm X" in the *Los Angeles Review of Books* and he has published peer-reviewed scholarship in several academic venues. He serves as guest editor for the Oxford African-American Studies Center with a focus on improving its archive of California scholarship. Keenan received a 2017 Marin Headlands Artist-in-Residence fellowship. He teaches American literature and creative writing at San Jose State.

VANESSA NUNEZ is a graduate student in the California State University of San Bernardino's English Master's Program. She has a B.A. in English, Creative Writing, and Media and Cultural Studies from the University of California, Riverside. When not writing, she reads comic books, watches horror and science fiction films, and plays video games. She is a San Bernardinian and this is her first published piece of fiction.

MICHAEL ORLICH is a physician and researcher who currently resides in Colton, but has lived in San Bernardino. He and his wife Raewyn have a 1-year-old daughter, Eleanor, and another baby on the way. He hosts a monthly poetry group in his home and has organized a new series of quarterly poetry readings at Loma Linda University.

JULIE SOPHIA PAEGLE is the author of *torch song tango choir* and *Twelve Clocks* (University of Arizona Press). Her poetry has been widely published and anthologized, and her books have won recognition in the International Latino Book Awards (in the category of Best Poetry in English) and in *Poets & Writers* (for one of the best debuts of 2010). She is Professor of English at Cal State San Bernardino, where she has directed the M.F.A. program in Creative Writing. She lives in the San Bernardino mountains with her family.

ROBERT PORTER is a 4th Generation business owner living in San Bernardino. He is an educated trained anthropologist that loves art and San Bernardino with all his heart.

ORLANDO RAMIREZ graduated from Yale University, then 25 years later earned his MFA from the Cal State San Bernardino Creative Writing program. He has been published in numerous small magazines and, although he is retired from his career as a newspaper editor, he continues to write poetry.

LINDA RAVENSWOOD is a poet and a performance artist from Los Angeles. She is the founder and editor in chief of The Los Angeles Press. Her work has been commissioned by The Los Angeles County Museum of Art, The Los Angeles Municipal Art Gallery, Google, The Broad Theater, Santa Monica Museum of Art, The New York Society Library, The Library Foundation of Los Angeles, and many other corporate and civic partners including The Department of Cultural Affairs, The Television

Critics Association, and The Emmy Awards. She is the winner of the 2019 California Writers Project, two times a finalist for Poet Laureate of West Hollywood, and shortlisted for Poet Laureate of Los Angeles 2017. She is a teaching artist for the 24th Street Theatre in DTLA, and The Angels Gate Cultural Arts Center in San Pedro. She visits upwards of 65 schools annually in the LAUSD and surrounding districts. In 2020 she is adjunct professor at Vanderbilt University. Her full collection of poetry *rock waves / slow drags* forthcoming from Eyewear London.

DANE RIGBY is a San Bernardino native. His story is excerpted from his memoir about growing up in San Bernardino.

CINDY RINNE creates fiber art and writes in San Bernardino, CA. She was Poet in Residence for the Neutra Institute Gallery and Museum, Los Angeles, CA. She has created fiber art for over 30 years, exhibiting internationally. Cindy collaborates in Performance Poetry using her own costume creations based on her books. A Pushcart nominee. Cindy is the author of several books: *Knife Me Split Memories* (Cholla Needles Press), *Letters Under Rock* with Bory Thach, (Elyssar Press), *Moon of Many Petals* (Cholla Needles Press), and others. Her poetry appeared or is forthcoming in: *Anti-Herion Chic, Unpsychology Magazine, MORIA,* several anthologies, and others. www.fiberverse.com

JESSIE SALAZAR is an incoming MFA student to San Jose State University. She received a bachelor's degree in Human Communication from California State University Monterey Bay. She is a nerdy, millennial lesbian from the Inland Empire, who loves interactive media, graphic design, and writing.

Born in Los Angeles and raised in the Inland Empire, IRENE SANCHEZ, PH.D. is a Xicana teacher, poet, and writer. After graduating from Rubidoux High School in Jurupa Valley CA, she attended Riverside City

College before transferring to UC Santa Cruz where she earned her B.A. in Latin American/Latino Studies and Sociology. She went on to earn a M.Ed. and Ph.D. in Educational Leadership and Policy Studies from the University of Washington-Seattle. Returning home after graduate school to Southern CA, Irene now teaches the only Chicano/Latino Studies course at three high schools everyday in the Azusa Unified School District. Dr. Sanchez was selected for the National Humanities Center Teacher Advisory Council for the 2019-2020 school year where she is the only teacher from California and only Ethnic Studies teacher on the 20-member council. A VONA and Pink Door Writers retreat alum, Irene is an award wining poet/writer, teacher, public scholar, and author of the blog "Xicana Ph.D.". Irene is the host of the monthly open mic Poetry y Pan at Cafe con Libros in Pomona, CA where she now serves on their Board of Directors as Chair of Literacy Projects. Her work has appeared in CNN, HuffPost, Public Radio International, Zocalo Public Square, Inside Higher Ed and more. She has been featured by multiple public radio outlets including KPCC, KPFK, NPR Latino USA, and ProPublica. For more information see `www.irenesanchezphd.com`

JULIE SCRIVNER moved to the Inland Empire from San Diego, CA in 1994 to attend UC Riverside and has lived in the region ever since. She currently lives in San Bernardino, CA where she has been an archaeologist and environmental planner for multiple state and federal agencies. She spends her free time painting, drawing, printmaking, and hiking the deserts and mountains of San Bernardino County with her husband, Seth. She attended UC Riverside, receiving a B.S. and M.A. in anthropology, and is a mostly self-taught artist who explores themes related to ecology, humanity's relationship to the natural world, and metaphorical understandings of nature through naturalistic and surrealistic imagery.

Romaine Washington, M.Ed. is the author of a collection of poems, *Sirens in Her Belly*, (Jamii Publishing). She is a published educator and a facilitator for the San Bernardino Inlandia Writing Workshop. She is also a fellow of the Inland Area Writing Project, U. C. Riverside and The Watering Hole, South Carolina. Ms. Washington resides in San Bernardino County and is an active participant in literary events. www.romainewashington.com.

Acknowledgments

Anderson, Cynthia: "The I-10" previously published in *Inlandia: A Literary Journey*, 2011.

Ayón, Erika: Poems previously published in her collection, *Orange Lady*, World Stage Press, 2018.

Coachbuilder, Deenaz: "The Tooth Fairy" was previously published in *Metal Horse and Shadows: A soul's Journey;* "The Runt Tree" was previously published in *International Center for Landscape and Language*, Edith Cowan University, Mount Lawley, Western Australia.

Free, Sheela Sitaram: "Uvulaic Rhapsody" and "San Bernardino Passion" previously published in her collection *Of Fractured Clocks, Bones and Windshields* (Plain View Press, 2009).

López, Casandra: "Fourth of July: San Bernardino Summer 2015" previously published in *The Feminist Wire.* "When Later Sounds Like Love"previously published in *The Tower Journal.*

Norris, Keenan: Excerpted from *Brother and the Dancer* (Heyday Books, 2013).

Rinne, Cindy: Acknowledged references for the poem, "Three Drops Balanced on an Elm Leaf - a Flame-singed Tip": *Kuan Yin* by Daniela Schenker; *Chinatown in San Bernardino* by Nicholas R. Cataldo; *The Luck of Third Street: Archaeology of Chinatown, San Bernardino, California* by Julia G. Costello, Kevin Hallaran, Keith Warren, and Margie Akin; *Historical Archaeology* (Vol. 42, No. 3, The Archaeology of Chinese Immigrant and Chinese American Communities (2008), pp. 136-151)

Scrivner, Julie: "Spring Joshua Tree" image courtesy of the artist. From the private collection of Ms. Cindy Brodie, Upland.

Washington, Romaine: "At the End of the Devil's Breath" previously published in *Voicemail Poems*, April 2018 and reprinted in *ACCOLADES: A Women Who Submit Anthology, 2020;* "Magnolia Estates" previously published in *Cholla Needles 32*, 2019.

About Inlandia Institute

Inlandia Institute is a regional non-profit and literary center. We seek to bring focus to the richness of the literary enterprise that has existed in this region for ages. The mission of the Inlandia Institute is to recognize, support, and expand literary activity in all of its forms in Inland Southern California by publishing books and sponsoring programs that deepen people's awareness, understanding, and appreciation of this unique, complex and creatively vibrant region.

The Institute publishes books, presents free public literary and cultural programming, provides in-school and after school enrichment programs for children and youth, holds free creative writing workshops for teens and adults, and boot camp intensives. In addition, every two years, the Inlandia Institute appoints a distinguished jury panel from outside of the region to name an Inlandia Literary Laureate who serves as an ambassador for the Inlandia Institute, promoting literature, creative literacy, and community. Laureates to date include Susan Straight (2010-2012), Gayle Brandeis (2012-2014), Juan Delgado (2014-2016), Nikia Chaney (2016-2018), and Rachelle Cruz (2018-2020).

To learn more about the Inlandia Institute, please visit our website at www.InlandiaInstitute.org.

Other Inlandia Books publications

Writing from Inlandia: Work from the Inlandia Creative Writing Workshops, an annual publication

Orangelandia: The Literature of Inland Citrus by Gayle Brandeis

Facing Fire: Art, Wildfire, and the End of Nature in the New West by Douglas McCulloh

In the Sunshine of Neglect: Defining Photographs and Radical Experiments in Inland Southern California, 1950 to the Present by Douglas McCulloh

Henry L. A. Jekel: Architect of Eastern Skyscrapers and the California Style by Dr. Vincent Moses and Catherine Whitmore

While We're Here We Should Sign by The Why Nots

No Easy Way: Integrating Riverside Schools - A Victory for Community by Arthur L. Littleworth

The Silk the Moths Ignore by Bronwen Tate
Winner of the 2019 National Hillary Gravendyk Prize

Remyth: A Postmodernist Ritual by Adam Martinez
Winner of the 2019 Regional Hillary Gravendyk Prize

Former Possessions of the Spanish Empire by Michelle Peñaloza
Winner of the 2018 National Hillary Gravendyk Prize

All the Emergency-Type Structures by Elizabeth Cantwell
Winner of the 2018 Regional Hillary Gravendyk Prize

Our Bruises Kept Singing Purple by Malcolm Friend
Winner of the 2017 National Hillary Gravendyk Prize

Traces of a Fifth Column by Marco Maisto
Winner of the 2016 National Hillary Gravendyk Prize

God's Will for Monsters by Rachelle Cruz
Winner of the 2016 Regional Hillary Gravendyk Prize
Winner of a 2018 American Book Award

Map of an Onion by Kenji C. Liu
Winner of the 2015 National Hillary Gravendyk Prize

All Things Lose Thousands of Times by Angela Peñaredondo
Winner of the 2015 Regional Hillary Gravendyk Prize

Go to the Living by Micah Chatterton